LEAD
US INTO
TEMPTATION

BREANDÁN Ó hEITHIR

LEAD US INTO TEMPTATION

Translated by the author from the Irish
Lig Sinn i gCathú

Routledge & Kegan Paul

London, Henley and Boston

First published in Irish in 1976
by Sáirséal agus Dill, Dublin, as
Lig Sinn i gCathú.
This English translation
first published in 1978
by Routledge & Kegan Paul Ltd
39 Store Street, London WC1E 7DD,
Broadway House, Newtown Road,
Henley-on-Thames, Oxon RG9 1EN and
9 Park Street, Boston, Mass. 02108, USA
Second Impression 1978
Set in 11/12 Baskerville by
Hope Services, Wantage
and printed in Great Britain by
Lowe & Brydone Ltd, Thetford, Norfolk
© this translation Breandán Ó hEithir 1978

British Library Cataloguing in Publication Data

Ó hEithir, Breandán

Lead us into temptation.
I. Title
891.6'2'34F   PB1399.0/   78-40586

ISBN 0 7100 0030 8

For Jim O'Halloran

THURSDAY

14

APRIL
1949

1

The rasping college clock struck three as Martin Melody walked slowly in the main gate. He had chosen the time carefully; although most of the students had gone home for Easter, the office staff stuck rigidly to official hours. The place was deserted except for the college porter, Patrick Purcell, who stood watching a small black dog burrowing a hole in a flower-bed opposite the archway under the clock-tower. Purcell was a large, surly, dark-skinned fellow with an enormous belly. He was called the Pooka behind his back. In his youth he had fought in the War of Independence and joined the Free State Army when it was founded. His service in the Civil War got him his job of porter at the University but no sooner was he established in the post than a miraculous conversion occurred and he became the chief tormentor of the Blue-shirts of Ballycastle in the thirties.

The Pooka was urging on the dog for all he was worth. 'Sa-ha-ha, doggie! Good Bran!' The little dog growled happily and the Pooka threw him a bone.

'Sa-ha-ha doggie!' he called and glanced towards the stone bungalow directly inside the main gate where the gardener lived. He noticed Martin coming towards him and hailed him cordially. The Pooka was intimate with

1

all the students who spent more than a year in college, particularly those who frequented the local pubs.

'By God, Melody! The dead arose and appeared to many. It's a long time since I dipped my moustache in a pint you bought. I heard it said you had taken the Holyhead boat!'

The porter threw another little bone to the dog and walked into the archway. Just then a howl of rage came from the gardener's cottage as the gardener saw what was happening. He was a small stocky man without any visible neck between head and shoulders and showing every sign that the next paroxysm of rage might well bring on a heart attack. His breath came in gasps and one could hear grunts of, 'May you drown and smother' — 'May you be violated!' As soon as the dog heard him he took off, bones in mouth, around the corner of the building to the house of his master, the President.

Bran and the flower-beds were part of a state of war which had existed since 1933. One night in the autumn of that year the Pooka returned to the University after an expedition out the country where he had beaten up some Blueshirts who were trying to run a dance. He had his fill of drink taken and found the little wicket gate bolted on the inside. From that point on there are two versions of the story but, as the gardener was an unrepentant Free Stater and a member of the Blueshirts, the Pooka smelt politics. He pulled loose stones out of the college wall and let fly through the windows of the cottage.

The gardener had to get one of the children out through a back window to call the police but by the time they arrived there wasn't a whole pane of glass in the house and the gardener, his wife and children were lying under the beds, terrified. Despite the efforts of the college authorities the case went to court. The gardener and his wife swore that they were still shattered by the event and that never again would they sleep a peaceful wink if the Pooka wasn't bound over to keep the peace. The court ruled that the Pooka must never again speak to the gardener or any member of his family. The administrative council of the college reinforced this judgment unanimously and but for the fact that the college Republican Club (who were madly seeking any kind of martyr at the time) threatened disruption the Pooka would surely have been fired.

The spite smouldered in the Pooka's heart from year to year but when Monsignor Blake and his little dog, Bran, took up residence in college, he found a way around the law. Monsignor Blake became President by accident and as a result of the kind of compromise that was commonplace in the college. The two who were really in line for the position differed politically but it also happened, by a curious quirk, which couldn't occur again for ten generations, that they were both lukewarm about religion and independent of the clergy. Father Blake was a junior lecturer in Welsh and didn't interfere much in college affairs or in academic affairs either. He usually accepted one student a year to ensure continuity of tenure but got rid of anyone who showed too much enthusiasm for his subject. He spent his free time in the lounge of the Railway Hotel drinking whiskey and chatting lightheartedly with whoever came his way.

He was approaching middle age and already showing signs of senility when Bishop Mullins sent for him one day and ordered him to set off around the province to canvass for the presidency. This he did, as he would have obeyed any other conceivable instruction from the bishop. But it was his day of doom. When he returned from his pilgrimages to the town and county councillors of the province he was an out-and-out drunk. He was made monsignor shortly after his appointment in the hopes that elevation might conceal his idiocy, but to no avail. When one woman in the town heard of it she exclaimed: 'Glory be to God, but the poe is on the dresser now with a vengeance!' A short time later the bishop appointed his secretary as an assistant to look after him; thus the bishop took complete control of the University.

Ten years had passed since these events but Monsignor Blake had not changed much apart from a deepening of his

3

dotage. During conferring, in the previous autumn, he tried hard to press a diploma in medicine on a photographer from the *Ballycastle Courier* who was standing near him in the Aula Maxima taking pictures. His only constant companions were his fat little dog, Bran, and the two bottles of whiskey he emptied daily. On the really bad days he didn't recognise anyone, not even the dog. He often hunted him out of the little private garden at the back of the college, shouting, 'Get out, you bitch! Go home, you bitch!' although it was a dog. Some of the academic staff laid bets on the likelihood of Bran getting a complete nervous breakdown as he never knew whether to expect a kick or a caress from his master. It was during one of his master's bouts of confusion that he first arrived in the Pooka's nook in the archway where he sought sanctuary from some engineering students who were trying to hit him in the eyes with lighted cigarette butts. The Pooka discovered that the lonely little dog could be taught a variety of tricks and from then on he was at war with the gardener's flowerbeds. It was hard to imagine the inordinate delight which this vendetta afforded the staff.

'Your scholarship cheque is in the Bursar's office,' said the Pooka. 'Whatever the hell caused the terrible delay? Didn't the rest of them get paid around St Brigid's Day?'

The Pooka knew full well what caused the delay. He also knew that Martin had not frequented the place very much since Christmas and that the scholarship cheque which had now arrived was one withheld during the previous term. The message on the card was as dry and laconic as the man who dictated it. 'Come at your convenience.'

'I must face Balor of the Evil Eye,' said Martin. Like most of the staff and indeed most of the population of Ballycastle, the Bursar had a nickname which was in far more common use than his proper one. The Pooka said what he always said on such occasions: 'Look him between the two eyes and tell him to go to hell.'

Martin crossed the small grass quadrangle in the centre of the college buildings and knocked on the office door.

The clatter of a typewriter stopped and he heard the Bursar's secretary calling on him to come in. She was a small, shy woman, much loved by everyone.

'Good day, Martin. Wait a moment and I'll get himself for you.'

Martin waved a hand at her and said in a whisper, 'Can't you slip it to me yourself? I don't really want. . . .'

She shook her head in a friendly and compassionate way.

'He has the cheque himself, I think he wants to speak to you. For God's sake now, Martin, don't say anything. . . .' She put her forefinger to her lips and went towards the door of the inner office. She opened it and murmured something.

'I'll be with him directly,' said the Bursar in a loud and surly voice, his chair moved suddenly and he came slowly into the front office. He was a tall angular man who had suffered a stroke on his right side in middle age which left him slightly lopsided and affected one eye. It was very difficult to address him directly as this eye wandered all over the place while the other one stared directly at you. He came towards Martin holding the cheque between forefinger and thumb as if it were soiled. Martin looked directly at the steady eye and made a great effort to ignore everything else in the room. The Bursar sighed impatiently and shook his head.

'I have no intention of dragging this out, Melody, I have no appetite for preaching sermons to people who won't obey sense and reason . . . and I know full well that you are one of them. You showed promise . . . you had promise . . . promise . . . yes, but what did you do then?' The Bursar threw his hands in the air and the cheque floated away dangerously towards the fire. The little secretary got to her feet, caught it safely and trotted happily towards the Bursar. Martin sought to turn the action to his advantage: 'You'll get your place back on the county team, Miss Kennedy!'

She implored him with a frightened glance but the Bursar groaned, snapped the cheque out of her hand and hit the office counter with his open palm.

'Blather!' he said, 'Blather and nonsense! What kind of a fool are you at all? You certainly didn't take after your brother. . . . I don't know what's to be done with you.'

The start he got caused Martin to lose his grip on the constant eye and fall into the confusion of the one that was now careering all over the office. He was afraid of being overcome with laughter and tried to concentrate his mind on his pressing problems which were far from being a laughing matter. But suddenly he remembered a story about a missionary in the tropics who was about to flog his servant for thieving and who accompanied his preparations with a sermon. The servant said: 'If you flogee, flogee. If you preachee, preachee. But no flogee and preachee too.' The tiny germ of humour was sufficient to make Martin gasp with foolish laughter. It was his undoing. The secretary stopped typing and clasped her head in her hands. The Bursar placed his two hands on the counter and bowed his head. There was a ghastly silence. Just as Martin decided to apologise the Bursar slapped the cheque down in front of him, pointed a finger at him and said with great deliberation: 'Take it! That is the second instalment from last term . . . thirty-four pounds, seven shillings and sixpence. The Government will not pay another penny because of your absence from almost all your lectures during this term. Unless you have 100 per cent attendance at your lectures next term there is very little chance that you will be allowed to sit for your degree. But for the excuses that were made, because of your father's illness, you wouldn't even be getting this. It's not the policy of the Department of Education to supply drinking money to cornerboys who don't see fit to come into the college at all.'

Anger swelled in Martin. 'I didn't ask anyone to drag my father's illness into this. I didn't want. . . .'

'That ends the matter. Take the money. I may as well tell you also that your brother knows about this. He came to me and I told him. I regard him highly. I regard him very highly.'

You would, you cockeyed old cadaver, said Martin to

6

himself, seeing as how himself and your lout of a son were ordained together in Maynooth and let loose to trample on decent people. He picked up the cheque and walked away without a word. He heard Miss Kennedy's voice: 'Good luck to you, Martin.'

'And to you too, Miss Kennedy!'

The Pooka was standing in the middle of the archway waiting for him. Martin was not in the mood for wasting time but before he came near him at all the Pooka let a screech out of him.

'It seems that poor Emmet will have to wait; for all that that will worry the robbers that are milking the country dry. Republic be damned . . . that's the Republic that was cheaply bought. The curse of Christ on the whole lot of them. Lawyers and old Blueshirts all as crooked as a ram's horn. Ah, my poor Robert Emmet! Your epitaph won't be written on Monday!'

Martin then realised that the Pooka was talking about the Republic of Ireland which was to be declared officially on Easter Monday and that his remarks were directed at the gardener's back as he repaired the damage to his flower-beds with a trowel. Martin waved his cheque, murmured something about banking hours and the Easter weekend and debts and slipped out past the Pooka. He hadn't gone very far, however, when he heard the big man's heavy trot behind him.

'Hey, Martin, I won't keep you a minute!' He caught him by the arm, lowered his voice and asked: 'How is he, Martin?'

'My father? There is not a lot of hope for him, to tell the truth, not much hope at all. He's not improving anything, I'm afraid.' And God forbid you should ask me when I saw him last.

'God help us! He's earning it, the poor man.'

'He has no pain, as far as he says himself, but he is wasting away under the bedclothes. That's the way. Look, I'll have to run. I might see you in town tonight and stand you that pint. . . .'

As Martin walked out the main gates he sud nly remembered his first days as a University student and how proud he felt. Keeping such thoughts out of his mind or banishing them quickly from his mind were his main mental occupations in recent times. He had various ways of getting rid of them: some more effective than others. At this moment he concentrated his mind on the bank; on the necessity for getting his hands on money immediately; on how he would have to meet his brother later on. . . . And as this last thought caused further darts of doubt to assail him he snorted and said to himself: 'I have thirty odd pounds and to hell with lawful debts!'

'I beg your pardon Martin? What's that you said?' asked the girl who was standing at a gate on the other side of the road. As often happened when his mind was wrestling with unpleasant thoughts, he must have spoken aloud. He stood and smiled his shy dishonest smile.

'I'm rushing down to the bank. If I don't catch it today it won't be open again until the middle of next week.'

He began to wave his hands in the air and tried to escape but she bore down on him across the road. It's really my day, he said to himself, and how lucky that I am really rushing. This was Imelda O'Connor whose father was Professor of Engineering in the University. She was in the same year as Martin but was studying medicine and had an active interest in about five other subjects. She couldn't be described as either pretty or plain. She was president of the college praesidium of the Legion of Mary, a task she took very seriously.

'I'm heading in that direction myself as it so happens. Are you going home this evening or do you intend working on until Easter Saturday? You're doing your degree in autumn aren't you?'

'O'Grady and myself are up to our necks in Anglo-Saxon verbs. . . .' I've said the wrong thing again, he said to himself, and she bloody well thinks it was deliberate. Billy O'Grady was his lodging and drinking companion in recent times and some months previously, the night the college

8

team won the Fitzgibbon Cup for hurling, O'Grady was at the celebrations full of free drink. As he passed by the room where the Legion held their meetings he heard the sound of prayers. Sticking his member through the letter-box in the door he let fly, as he put it himself, a spout of piss on to the floor. Had he indecently assaulted the assembled praesidium the event could hardly have caused greater furore. A full official enquiry was held and although all and sundry knew O'Grady was the culprit there were no witnesses to the happening. Some of the girls had seen the offending object but as O'Grady himself said, 'They weren't the type of women who should be able to distinguish my weapon and another', and for this and other reasons the enquiry was dropped. The wound was still raw as was clear now from Imelda O'Connor's face, but she decided to be sensible about it.

'I wouldn't think that Anglo-Saxon verbs had a great attraction for Mr O'Grady, but never mind stupidities. I want to ask you a question. Why didn't you sign the petition for the release of Cardinal Mindszenty? Now don't tell me that you weren't in college. Maureen Maguire told me she stopped you up at the Square and that you said . . . .'

'I said my opinion didn't matter a damn east of the Iron Curtain and that we ought to busy ourselves with matters closer to home. That's all I said.'

They were on the bridge that spanned the junction of the river and the lake which lay north of Ballycastle, one of the loveliest spots in the town; which was probably why the bishop planned to build a cathedral there which would measure up to his own opinion of his importance in the eyes of God and man. Martin often spent hours leaning over the parapet watching the salmon as they lay there before moving up to the lake. Imelda placed a friendly hand on his arm.

'Easy, Martin, easy! We should discuss these matters . . . *discuss* them you understand. It serves no purpose to get heated.'

Her hand is lingering on my arm! Had another good girl

9

been beguiled by the blue eyes, the thin pale face, the aimless gait. He was just about to direct an obscenity over the Iron Curtain towards Mindszenty's prison cell when Imelda removed her hand and began to rebuke him as she walked briskly on.

'I understand what you mean! You may think that strange but I was once like that. Now I call the disease "the Sinn Féinism of the soul". One could argue about the effect of ultra-nationalism . . . but that's another matter.'

She was now in top gear and Martin remembered college debates and the discussions which followed them. Her hands wove patterns in the air and her laboured breathing reminded him of Billy O'Grady's women (if his accounts could be believed) when they craved the rod. She spoke in gusts.

'I was always pious. I was a daily communicant . . . every day . . . but that I regarded as a private matter . . . between myself and God alone . . . that part of my life, you understand? It never occurred to me that this was something I held in partnership with others. But my last year in school . . . during retreat . . . silence and all that you understand. . . . Well! I picked up this booklet by the Legion's founder, Frank Duff, and I read that one billion and three hundred million people, would never, never. . . .' She stood and pointed a finger at him. 'A billion, three hundred million! Just think of it . . . all over the world . . . they will never have the opportunity of ever receiving Holy Communion . . . and why? . . . because Christ was never brought to them as He was to you and to me. . . . There's your Sinn Féinism!'

The incomprehensible figure was imbedded in Martin's brain. But what had all this to do with Cardinal Mindszenty? She didn't wait to be asked.

'Your neighbour, Martin Melody, is the human race in its totality, without exception, even those who harm you.'

They had come into the square in front of the bank. They stood and again Imelda placed a friendly hand on his arm.

'Believe me, Martin, I do enjoy debating with you. A pity that you abandoned the intellectual life of college . . . a temporary lapse, I do hope. And another thing . . . we in the Legion are not narrow-minded and witless . . . we do our best . . . we only lack support . . . the likes of yourself indeed . . . and Martin . . . I wish you a happy Easter!'

She walked away happily across the square. She would get first-class honours and a job in college and perhaps a chair and without a doubt she would make a good wife for someone. Martin turned quickly as he heard the creaking of the bank door as it was being shut. He ran up the steps and slipped in to beat the long Easter closure.

2

It was often said that Ballycastle never made up its mind whether to become a country town or remain a medieval city. One of the reasons for this was the medieval remains still prominent in the centre of town. Two of the old gates still survived, albeit in a dilapidated condition, as did the remains of business houses from the sixteenth and seventeenth centuries. There was a spacious square in the centre of town and near it the Cathedral with a clock that was visible from a great distance. But Ballycastle wasn't too happy with the Cathedral. It was old and full of history but it belonged to the Protestants; a small community which had dwindled so rapidly that it was now sad to see them huddled in their vast Cathedral, their voices, drowned by the organ, echoing among the lofty beams.

In a narrow alleyway off Middle Street stood the Catholic Pro-Cathedral, a large neutral limestone building more like a granary than a church. It was rumoured that the Protestant Bishop had offered his cathedral to Bishop Mullins in a straight swop for the Pro-Cathedral. Bishop Mullins turned down the offer curtly saying that he would much prefer the roof to come down on his opposite number, as it surely would due to advanced dry-rot in the beams. There the matter rested but certainly the Cathedral badly needed repairing and the more knowledgeable among the public gave the clock-tower a wide berth when more than four strokes were expected. And shortly after the offer was made (if indeed it was ever made) it was announced in the most official way that a brand new Catholic Cathedral was to be built between the University and the river. No further information was given but again rumour had it that every Catholic in the diocese would have to subscribe a half-crown a week for ten years to clear the cost. As most of the population of the diocese lived in Ballycastle this rumour did little to cheer them up, particularly since they had been heavily levied a short time before to prop up Maynooth College and keep it from falling into the Royal Canal. But the money was sure to be collected and the Cathedral built and everyone would say publicly that it was beautiful and privately that it was a monstrous waste of money and that Christ was born in a stable.

The ancient narrow streets in the centre of Ballycastle went around in irregular curves and circles which drove visitors to distraction as they seemed to be trapped in a medieval maze; always finishing exactly where they started.

But once you left the centre of town all roads led to the country. Indeed, some streets entered the country so suddenly that one could take leave of a friend in a suburban road, turn a corner and find oneself in a field of horses, sheep or cows.

The town was eating into the countryside and the countryside seemed to be resisting the town. Across the river which cut Ballycastle in two was Irishtown, perched high on a bank overlooking the bay. It was here the Irish lived when English and Anglo-Irish ruled the town. At present, due to constant emigration, most of the population of Irishtown were employed in England. The Irishtown fishing fleet had a long history but under native government it dwindled and vanished and those who wished to pursue the heritage of the sea had to join the British Navy, as many of them did. People didn't talk

12

about this very much in Ballycastle or anywhere else either.

About a mile west of Ballycastle lay a small seaside resort which was crammed with tourists for three months of the year and dismally deserted for the other nine. It was called Golden Strand and since the end of the war it was said that in summertime randy women were more numerous there than the grains of sand on the beach. This was probably the usual Ballycastle exaggeration and at any rate the strand was only a few yards long. There was a campaign in progress to remove the loose rocks from the rest of the beach and provide more sunning-space for the hundreds from Britain and Northern Ireland who came to gorge themselves on food, drink and willing human flesh.

Between Irishtown and Golden Strand stretched Stella Maris Road, a long straggle of houses of different shapes and sizes. It was completed before the war and was the pride of the middle classes. If the rest of the population shared their pride they kept it to themselves. Its birth was orderly until the time came to christen it. As usual the town divided politically. The Fianna Fáil Party wanted it called Éamon de Valera Road and the Fine Gael Party favoured Liam Cosgrave Road. The two parties had the same number of seats on the town council but Fianna Fáil had the Chair as a result of a deal done with the lone Labour councillor, who was promised a job as an insurance agent, and an Independent Republican who hated de Valera's guts and who abstained. These two ruled the council and they held the balance on this occasion as well. They told Fianna Fáil that they would willingly accept James Connolly Road and they were sure that Fine Gael could hardly oppose it. They also said that it would be a good thing to decide a matter of such importance for the town unanimously. But while these talks were taking place in a back room in the Royal Hotel, leading businessmen were meeting the Fine Gael members in an even more discreet room in the Knights of Columbanus Club. These important citizens said that squabbling was unseemly and that unanimity in a matter of such importance was desirable.

13

They also said that the political parties should agree on a name completely divorced from politics which would be acceptable to the majority of citizens. The new road skirted the bay, there was widespread devotion to the Blessed Virgin in Ballycastle, therefore, why not Stella Maris Road? Without any doubt it was highly acceptable. Numerous large whiskies were downed and there was much laughter at the predicament in which Fianna Fáil now found themselves.

At this stage Fianna Fáil had totally accepted James Connolly as a sainted patron of their own. Then they were hit by an ecclesiastical bullet. On the Friday evening, just before the decisive meeting, the *Ballycastle Courier* published a list of resolutions which had been passed by sodalities, pioneers, scapular wearers, First Friday and Daily Communicants Associations, at a series of meetings, asserting that the majority of citizens wished the new road to be called Stella Maris Road. There was also a letter from 'Catholic Mother, Golden Strand' (name and address with Editor), which declared that it would be nothing less than a studied insult to the Blessed Virgin to name the road after 'one who was to the fore in promoting the alien and poisonous plant of Socialism on Irish soil'. Fianna Fáil were crushed and surrendered without firing a shot. They were followed by the poor lackey from the Labour Party who delivered a speech in which he gave the lie to rumours concerning James Connolly's last hours. He denied categorically that Connolly had consigned to Hell's flames the priest who came to hear his last confession and who as a consequence refused him absolution. He said the council's decision would have gladdened Connolly's heart as it was common knowledge that he constantly prayed to the Virgin Mary for guidance during the glorious Easter Rising.

Only Martin MacInerney, the old Republican, stood firm. He called the others a shameless gang of hypocrites and said that if the Fine Gael councillors were true to their political and business principles they would have called the road Judas Iscariot Road. This part of his speech was not reported in the local paper but it appeared curiously in an English Sunday paper under the heading 'HE WOULD PREFER JUDAS TO THE BLESSED VIRGIN'. By this time the road was christened, the name-plates put up at both ends and the furore all but dead when an event occurred which clearly showed that God was having a keen eye to His Blessed Mother's standing in Ballycastle. Because of frustration, disgust and a fortnight's binge, MacInerney decided to re-christen the road. He got a bucket of tar and a brush and at dead of night began to daub and write. He had only obliterated one name-plate and scrawled 'CONN . . .' on the wall beneath when he was set upon and left with a broken leg and a gash in his head that took sixteen stitches to close. It was said that a lunatic on a motor cycle had hit him and matters were left at that. It had to be a sign from God; although those who were in the know said that God had chosen strange messengers, three MacDonagh brothers from Irishtown who were settling an old score with MacInerney: an unfinished fight that took place many years before during a Republican vendetta against British ex-servicemen. It was all history now except that MacInerney still limped slightly and the MacDonaghs were known in Irishtown as 'Mary's Army'.

Martin Melody lodged in number 107 Stella Maris Road. It had been named *Pacelli* some years previously by Mrs Anderson, a middle-aged widow who bought it with the insurance money she and her four children received after her husband, a police detective, finally succeeded in calcifying his liver with whiskey. Mrs Anderson was small and pasty-faced and whined constantly and disapprovingly through her nose. She was exceedingly pious and kept a weather-eye constantly open for transgressions which might draw the wrath of God on her 'little holy family', as she called it. Apart from discussing her neighbours' concealed vices which she skilfully detected and broadcast in the form of parables designed to save the hearers from damnation, she had few topics of conversation except religion. She was a member of every guild, sodality

15

and religious association in the town. Her house was visited by a stream of priests, unravelling her problems, advising her on the education of her family and suggesting the various religious orders where she could lodge them safely away from the wicked world. She was also visited by a stream of policemen on night-duty who came to drink tea. These visitations began as a kind of obligation towards a dead comrade and later, when they might have a drink or two taken, to find out if she was being affected by compulsory abstinence from the pleasures of her marriage bed. But Mrs Anderson was safe from such assaults on her virtues. She replied with a sickening sanctimoniousness calculated to scupper the most maniacal lust. They returned for the tea and to swap the secrets of police-station and town.

As befitted the widow of a dipsomaniac, Mrs Anderson had a particular understanding of drink and its problems. It also suited her to describe it as 'a decent man's weakness'. But she was constantly in pursuit of impurity in word or deed. This was the cardinal sin for it seemed that Sergeant Anderson was too busy knocking back booze to set his sights beyond his lawful spouse. The boarders in *Pacelli* conformed to Mrs Anderson's desires: students who wanted peace and minor clerks who sought respectability of address and location. But these were almost always accompanied by some students who needed shelter and sanctuary which were also available on the terms laid down by Mrs Anderson who dearly loved to lead transgressors from the path of sin. And when her boarders denigrated Mrs Anderson for her bad food, her nagging, her sickly piety, her nosiness and other shortcomings, they always admitted that she possessed a streak of charity which made up for some of them; even though it was a charity that reluctantly left the home where it began.

At seven o'clock on Holy Thursday evening Mrs Anderson was sitting by the window of the dining-room looking out on Stella Maris Road and talking to Martin's companion, Billy O'Grady. Billy was sitting by the grate, which was known to contain a fire during fierce east winds and frost, reading a medical textbook belonging to a Polish student who had gone to England for Easter. He was listening with half an ear to Mrs Anderson as he studied the symptoms of venereal disease. It was past tea-time but as only Martin and himself remained in residence Mrs Anderson refused to wet tea twice.

'What on earth could be keeping him but that maybe he got that cheque at last and cashed it. . . . There's Pakie Green's daughter! And her mother saying she'd gone into the Louis Convent in Monaghan. Look at that skirt, and Lord save us! You can't believe a word you hear nowadays. But about Easter, Billy, I have to talk straight now. Billy, put away that book! I told Stan not to leave them where the children could get at them.'

Billy got up and put the book on the top shelf of the bookcase. He had just got out of bed and was hungry. He yawned and rubbed his palm over his pimples that were smarting after a shave with a new blade.

'Throw me my tea, Mrs Anderson, and don't mind him. If he has money he can get a bite up town. Don't you have to go down to the Dominicans soon?'

'The Jays tonight, Billy, a beautiful ceremony that I wouldn't miss for the world. Look Billy! Look who's coming! He's broken out again. Look at the cut of him!'

A tall man in a long black coat and a broadbrimmed black hat stood swaying on the footpath outside the window. He was escorted by two tattered men who were trying to propel him forward by the elbows. He was singing a ballad at the top of his voice and waving his walking stick. It was the Professor of Archeology and two casual dockers who had attached themselves to him during his rampage.

> We'll go down with our sh–i–i–i–p,
> Said the Cumberland's crew. . . .

'Musha, fair play to ye, Professor, auld stock!' said the dockers in encouragement. The procession moved slowly out of sight and earshot towards Golden Strand where the Professor lived.

'God between us and all harm but did you see the two latchicoes he has with him?' said Mrs Anderson. 'How does he hold on to the job at all?'

'He's no worse than most of the others but that he has the guts to do it in public,' said Billy.

The hall door was thrown open and Martin shot into the room. 'Did you see your man? Well you missed a right evening up in Maggie's, Billy, with your man buying and the house drinking. They were coming from all parts and there he was slapping fivers on the counter.'

Mrs Anderson sighed deeply and rose slowly from the armchair. She had a touch of rheumatism in the knees and walked with a roll like a sailor.

'I'll bring you the tea now. It's hardly worth while setting the table for two. You could be a little more punctual Martin, if you don't mind me saying so, but term is over and this isn't the Royal Hotel. Easy known your cheque came but remember that more than Maggie Fleming have call on it.'

'But I didn't get the cheque, Mrs Anderson. It was the Professor was buying.'

Mrs Anderson stopped dead in the kitchen door. Billy glanced at Martin, snatched a copy of *The Tempest* from the bookcase and began to read the preface. Mrs Anderson turned towards Martin wearing her idiotic smile.

'Your cheque didn't come? Is that what you're telling me? But how do you think I'm going to live? I'm a patient woman, Martin, but you owe me thirty pounds . . . thirty pounds tomorrow . . . ten clear weeks!'

Billy took his head out of the book, winked at Martin who was obviously tipsy and spoke casually to Mrs Anderson.

'You weren't listening to what he said, Mrs Anderson. He didn't say the cheque didn't come. He said he didn't get it. Who got it, Martin?'

'The brother, Father Brendan. Letters had come in about debts and the . . . the Bursar wouldn't give it to me. I'm meeting Father Brendan above in the Railway Hotel at nine . . . and . . . and. . . .' He waved his hands in the air and glanced at Billy who was smirking happily. You're improving, he thought to himself, two years ago you would have made a total mess of those lies. As soon as Mrs Anderson heard the priest's name she went into the kitchen and brought out the tea: six slices of bread, a bit of butter, a pot of tea and two previously fried eggs, dried out and stuck to the plates. She put the tray on the table in the middle of the room and said playfully: 'Butter away and eat up, there's plenty more where that came from.' Billy rose and surveyed their supper.

'Are you hungry, Mattie, auld skin?' Martin shook his head. Billy slipped a knife under one of the eggs and swallowed it whole. He then spread half the pat of butter on three slices of bread and wolfed them. He did the same with the other egg and the remaining bread and butter. Downing a cup of tea at one gulp he wiped his mouth with the back of his hand and said: 'May the giving hand never falter! Come on Martin, there are cows to be milked up the town!'

They were on their way out the door when Mrs Anderson called: 'One minute, Martin, a message for you.' She handed him an envelope. More trouble in our native land, he thought. Billy's watery eye had spotted it too and he cackled quietly.

'She waited half an hour but when you didn't turn up she left that for you. Don't be too late now and don't leave the lights on and don't forget the day that's in it tomorrow. For God's sake. And give Father Brendan my regards and tell him to call in some day.'

The two walked away from the house and down Stella Maris Road towards town. When they had passed out of Mrs Anderson's range Martin pulled two five pound notes out of his pocket and handed them to Billy.

'I very nearly made a mess of that business. It's not that I had all that much to drink but the pints were coming in half dozens at a time and then the whole lot of us were thrown out on the street when your man struck up "Take it down from the mast Free-State traitors".'

'He must have been bad when he started that in Maggie's.
I wouldn't mind but I thought of getting up and heading
that way about four but I dropped off again. . . .'

Billy would prefer the freezing frost to the thought of
losing free booze. He shook his head slowly like a footballer
who had missed an open goal.

'But listen to me, Martin, listen to me now. We're both
in trouble with this rattle-snake beyond but you're in right
trouble. We have to be gone before Monday evening at the
very latest . . . these bloody holy women are coming for
a conference . . . and where will you go and worse still,
what about the debts? You're up to the ears all over this
town. It's a good job you pulled the anointed brother out
of your hat or God only knows what she'd have done.'

'Look! Give over for Jesus' sake. Do you think I don't
know all this myself. She'll get her money. They'll all get
their money. Come on into the Atlantic Bar and buy me
a drink out of those debts I paid so honourably.'

They turned into a small pub near the bridge which
linked Stella Maris Road with the town centre, across the
river. It was a dark place and a lone customer sat drinking
a bottle of Guinness and chatting to the publican. He was a
schoolteacher who lived near their digs and was secretary
of the local branch of the Fianna Fáil party. As they came
in they could hear him holding forth on the declaration of
the Republic.

'I told the Chairman,' he said, 'straight up to his face.
"The whole bloody lot of us will go to the Mass and afterwards the whole bloody lot of us will go home. There's no
good at all in dragging religion into this but not a man Jack
of us will go up to that memorial on the square. Let them
have their sham republic if that's what they want!" Wasn't
I right?'

'It's no harm for anybody to go to Mass, no matter what
the intention behind the particular Mass might be. That's
my belief anyway.' And with that weighty comment off
his chest the publican poured two bottles of Guinness and
two half-whiskeys for Billy who was just about to hand

him a five pound note when he changed his mind and produced instead a fistful of small change and counted three shillings and ten pence.

'Have you tuppence there, Martin? Good man yourself.'

Martin went out to the evil-smelling little toilet at the back of the bar and pulled out the letter. Just as he feared!

Dearest Mattie,

You didn't come to me as you promised. We will have to have that chat tomorrow. Things here are bad again but if the two of us were all right I wouldn't mind so much. I will expect you tomorrow at 4.30 without fail, or if you prefer we can meet after the Stations of the Cross in the Dominicans. I'm depending on you. We can't go on like this. I'm very disturbed.

Lots of love,
Nuala

Martin threw the letter and the envelope into the toilet bowl and pulled the chain peevishly. When he went back to the bar O'Grady was shoving his own spoke into the discussion on the new Republic. He had an ability to give credibility to pronouncements on subjects about which he knew absolutely nothing. Now fully awake he was seeking whom he could plunder.

'Take Plato's republic,' he said. 'That meant total democracy, you understand?'

This categorical pronouncement annoyed the schoolmaster.

'Would you be trying to teach Éamon de Valera his business? Do you think he hasn't studied every republic on the face of the earth? Don't you see what is at the very heart of this matter?'

He was warming to his subject when O'Grady threw his knock-out punch.

'Making a game of something which people sacrificed their very lives for,' he said slowly and solemnly. 'That's the heart of the matter in my own humble and honest opinion.'

Martin gave him a nod, said he had to go and drained the bottle of Guinness. He passed the half-whiskey to Billy and made for the door.

'Wait a minute,' called the schoolmaster. 'Give the lads a drink! Wait till I tell ye about this Republic.'

Billy had hooked his fish. He told Martin he would see him later in the Lobster Pot and pulled his stool up close to the schoolmaster. The fivers would be spared, no doubt! Martin headed towards the Railway Hotel and his reverend brother. He had plenty of time but although he had picked up a lot of Billy's tricks he had no stomach for boring company, no matter how much free drink came with it. He also wanted to calm down and prepare for the unpleasant interrogation to which his brother was sure to subject him. He was still young in the practice of duplicity and deceit.

3

The lounge of the Railway Hotel was the most fashionable public place in Ballycastle in which to drink coffee or something stronger. It was here the monied classes met to display their social graces and the company they kept. The hotel was a square four-storey building that looked like a large limestone wedding-cake. Its smooth external characteristics were a reflection of what went on inside. The staff moved noiselessly to and fro on dark carpets, whispering discreetly. It was cut off completely from the noise and bustle of the outside world. Even the whistling of the trains in the adjoining station was barely heard inside. The furniture was heavy and ornate, the mirrors gilded, the dishes monogrammed and the customers either contented or trying hard to achieve that condition. This was the pinnacle of social life in Ballycastle.

When Martin came into the foyer, through the revolving doors, he found the hall-porter, Austin Sugrue, alone at his desk. This cute, soft-spoken Kerryman was one of the important personages of the town. At the age of fifteen he walked barefoot from Killarney to Ballycastle, a three-day journey, and offered his services to the manager of the hotel. He was set to work in the kitchen and in the thirty years that had since passed he had collected a deal of money and influence. His wife ran a large guest-house in Golden Strand and the cream of the customers who over-flowed from the Railway Hotel, during the high season, were channelled there. When petrol became more plentiful after the war Sugrue was the first man in town to rent cars by the day. Every carrot, slice of bacon and pint of milk that came under the roof carried a direct or indirect levy to his benefit. He was hated like poison in Ballycastle because he was a blow-in and because he managed, with single-minded impudence, to realise their own lazy fanta-sies of rapacity. They christened him 'empty fork' because he was childless but he cared little for their animosity. He was interested only in money.

He glanced professionally at Martin. Blue fisherman's jersey, shabby jacket, scuffed unpolished shoes, shiny trousers . . . looking for someone. He took off his glasses and recognised Martin.

'Mr Melody? The large lounge, right-hand corner inside the door. Many thanks.' He put on his glasses and forgot Martin instantly.

Father Brendan Melody sat in the corner deep in con-versation with two women in their early forties. When he saw his brother he put a hand behind his head, lay back in the armchair and clicked his fingers at a waitress who stood like a statue at the other end of the room. He beckoned to Martin and waved him towards an empty chair beside him. Martin sat down and looked at the two women who were chattering noisily and simultaneously about a charity ball which they were organising in the hotel to raise money for two families on the outskirts of the town who were being evicted for non-payment of rent.

'The Lord Mayor of Dublin and his wife will be guests of honour,' said Mrs Manning, the town clerk's wife, whose

23

life was a continuous round of social activity of a charitable nature.

'The two flocks . . . the two flocks . . . Protestant and Roman Catholic are working in complete harmony. Oh, it's marvellous.'

Mrs Maxwell, wife of the Reverend Maxwell, was a giddy and rather flighty woman and Father Brendan wasn't pleased with the way she gave precedence to her own flock and referred to his as *Roman* Catholics. But he laughed pleasantly and introduced his brother. They stood up and shook hands. Mrs Maxwell gave him a most cordial handshake and said she knew him to see, of course, and that he had the most beautiful blue eyes. He wasn't in the least interested in Mrs Manning but this was his first time meeting Mrs Maxwell. The cats of the town knew the Reverend Maxwell, a half-witted poor man who wandered about talking aloud to himself about chess. Before the war he had a little radio transmitter and played chess every night with people in all parts of the world. But when war broke out the police seized the set in case he broadcast information which might endanger Irish neutrality. It was said in Ballycastle that the loneliness upset the balance of his mind completely. But it wasn't because of this that Martin was interested in Mrs Maxwell but because he remembered meeting a housepainter late one night in the toilet of the Lobster Pot who told him, during a long relieving session, that he had seen the minister's wife stark naked on a bed rogering herself with a candle as he painted the eaves of the house. He found it difficult to imagine this giddy little woman stark naked and still more difficult. . . . Loosening the handclasp he sat down again. His brother pulled a face, said, 'God bless you and a Happy Easter', for a third time and turned to Martin. He was just about to speak when he remembered he had promised his mother not to start a row so he turned to the waitress who was standing patiently by his side and said, 'Coffee and . . . some scones . . . oven-fresh scones . . . for two please.'

You know full well I would like a drink but you just

24

won't give in with your Pioneer pin and your oven-fresh scones! But Martin also decided to keep his temper in check so with forced cheerfulness he asked, 'Mother? How's Mother? Killing herself working no doubt!'

Little you know about it, you shiftless little waster, was the answer to that one; but a promise was a promise.

'Worried! Worried! She doesn't sleep much. Work keeps her going . . . just as it keeps the rest of us going indeed. There is no cure for Dad . . . that much is clear . . . but how long . . . how long?'

He stretched out his arms in the form of a cross, shrugged his shoulders and then abruptly took out a packet of cigarettes and lit one. Martin saw that his brother was on the verge of tears and his heart gave an unexpected leap of compassion. Their father was dying; they had, after all, come from the same womb. The coffee arrived and this enabled them both to regain composure. And at that moment Martin decided that there was only one way out of his predicament. He was afraid that if an argument started he would lose control of himself. He didn't really know what he wanted to do but suspected that his mother and his brother had a definite course plotted for him. He decided to play along with it for the moment. When the coffee was poured the priest asked, as casually as he could, 'When are you coming home, Martin?'

'Will you come down on Sunday after the match and I'll go home with you? We can call in to see Dad on the way. . . .' He ran out of words and waved his hands in the air, realising for the first time that he shared his brother's nervous gestures. But did he believe him? The priest blew a jet of smoke through his nostrils and pondered. He took a deep breath and looked Martin straight in the eyes.

'I must admit you surprise me, surprise me greatly. I don't even believe you're sincere until I see proof. I must tell you I came here to put certain proposals to you . . . for the last time indeed . . . but these can wait until Sunday. What match is this that's so important?' His sarcasm was obvious for he knew Martin hadn't played a game of any kind since he left the regimented life of the diocesan college three years ago.

'The Republican Cup match between Brothers Pearse and Bawnmore. Canon Wallace put up the cup. It will be blue murder without a doubt.'

Father Brendan's face deliberately registered disgust. He didn't belong to the Ballycastle diocese and felt free to criticise. He shook his head and as the subject was a neutral one he spoke in a friendly way.

'I was always of the opinion, that the Catholic Church in Ireland should steer clear of the Gaelic Athletic Association and of all other sporting organisations as well. It is my considered opinion that Canon Wallace brings the Church into disrepute. Organising games is a matter for the laity. Look at the things that need to be done in this town: put an end to after-hours drinking, organise and supervise pastimes for those servant girls who roam the streets at night talking to soldiers, strengthen the Legion of Mary and the lay apostolate in general. Work! There is certainly no shortage of work to be done.'

The spark of affection which he felt earlier extinguished and gave way to deep loathing. Listen to him! Twenty-eight years of age and talking like that. Certainly, no one in Ballycastle could associate Canon Wallace with anything other than hurling no more than they could associate Monsignor Blake with anything other than whiskey and senility. But what really disturbed him was that anyone could be so self-satisfied and so dogmatic about everything as his brother was.

He rose suddenly and slapped his forehead.

'I nearly forgot! I was to meet the editor of the *Courier* and I'm late. I must run!'

He saw curiosity getting the better of suspicion in his brother's face. What was this feckless young brother of his up to now? Martin walked towards the door.

'He asked me to write a piece . . . a short essay really . . . on the history of republicanism in Ireland, giving information and a kind of background, you see.'

The priest walked beside him and put his arm over his shoulders with a patronising and self-satisfied smile.

'Well! Well! Won't mother be pleased. Well I hope that . . . while your ideas are your own of course . . . that you realise how we all loathe the gunmen and the kind of hero-worship they seemed to inspire. And the low esteem in which honest citizens are held. People who give employment. The thrifty man who gives good example and makes the country a better place.' He slapped Martin on the back. 'Congratulations! I'm glad to hear you have taken up the pen again. Yes indeed! That's the way the gifts are bestowed, you master words and I master figures. Good job for mother that I can. If this profession fails me I'll take up business!'

He laughed uproariously at his own joke and let Martin out the door ahead of him. It won't fail you, you miserable bastard, you'll have the best of both worlds! He looked at his brother's solid body, his fleshy neck, the full face that clearly showed years of over-eating. The priest was almost as tall as he was but because of his bulk looked inches shorter. A man of his age who led such a regular life must surely be subject to terrible temptations of the flesh? Or did they take something in their food to suppress the pangs? According to the folklore of boarding-school it was saltpetre mixed with the mashed potatoes that kept the seniors from mounting the servant girls or the junior boys. Martin snatched his thoughts off this dangerous course to hear his brother say, for the second time clearly, 'On Sunday then! Any time and place that suits?'

'Oh! Outside the Royal Hotel, about half-past four. I'll have left my bags there.'

'I'll be *inside* . . . in the lounge. I don't suppose it will be full of drunks at that hour of the day! God speed you. I'm calling in to see Dad on the way home.' And with that parting dart he walked across the square to his car. Martin stood watching him and concluded that he was about two stone over-weight for his age and build, although he didn't drink, and this thought gave him a little pleasure. But his

27

depression had returned and was beginning to deepen. He put his hand in the pocket where his money was and began to walk rapidly towards the centre of town.

4

There were two kinds of public house in Ballycastle: those that observed the licensing laws and those that didn't. Maggie Fleming's pub was on a corner across the street from the offices of the *Ballycastle Courier* and was frequented by its staff and the many people who did business with them. Maggie was a huge woman with about seven chins and calves like thighs. But she had grace and even beauty because of her deep musical voice and a serene and kindly countenance. She was only twenty when she inherited the pub from her aunt and was then so handsome that the place was always full of young men who were doing their best to get her into bed or into church. She treated them all in the same gentle way but none of them succeeded.

In the autumn of 1926 a girl in Berryfort, a tiny village four miles east of Ballycastle, saw the Blessed Virgin standing near a stream where the villagers came for water. Within days huge crowds, from all over the country, gathered in Berryfort until they nearly trampled the villagers into the ground in a stampede for miracles. The parish priest and Bishop Mullin were visiting Rome at the time and they put a quick end to the affair when they returned. The girl was shoved into the Presentation Convent with the unmarried mothers and kept there until she denied the validity of her vision. But before this happened Maggie's pub was full of newsmen from the more colourful British papers who were busily milking the story of 'The Virgin of the Fairy Fort' or 'Our Lady of the Berries' into acres of newsprint. Most of them had no religious beliefs whatever and spent their time in Maggie's collecting gossip and phoning it home from the *Courier* office.

Among these was a fragile little fellow with a long neck

28

and thin black moustache. He was one of Lord Beaver-brook's photographers and within two days Maggie was in love for the first time. The fellows who had spent so much time and money in their efforts to entice her were hurt and horrified. Only their genuine affection for her prevented them from drowning the skinny little Englishman in the river. It was a heart-scald for them to leave the pub at closing time knowing the persuasive little man would stay behind. Then it was reported (the walls of Ballycastle having eyes as well as ears) that the photographer was seen walking bow-legged from Maggie's to the Royal Hotel at six in the morning; a report which was confirmed by the loose-mouthed hotel porter. It was hard to credit it but the little Englishman was slipping it to Maggie. A tick on a cow's belly, said those who were able to salve their anger with sarcasm. But they had to put up with it. And when the Bishop returned from Rome, even before he imprisoned the girl who had presumed to see the Blessed Virgin while his back was turned (and in such a miserable place to boot) he ordered the villagers to rout the British press.

To prove the strength of their renewed allegiance to the faith, the people of Berryfort caught the little photographer and a reporter from the *Daily Mail* who had gone to the place against all advice and beat them to a pulp. A stone wall was knocked on top of the photographer and only the prompt arrival of Sergeant Lynch on his bicycle saved him from drowning in the blessed stream. He spent two months in hospital in Ballycastle before being taken in plaster to London where his wife and children were waiting anxiously for him.

About nine months after these events a baby girl was born to Maggie who christened her Sal. It was the end of romance also, for as well as being plain to the point of ugliness Sal was also simple-minded. But Maggie kept her customers happy as before with her gentle and generous ways and soft musical voice. And in the mysterious way that such things happened in Ballycastle someone found that various liberties could be taken with Sal, or she could be waylaid unknown to her mother (which wasn't easy) in the long, dark passageway between the bar and the back-yard toilet. Because of this she was christened Salamander and although Maggie never gave a hint of being aware of the risks her daughter ran, she ceased having people in after hours and kept Sal indoors after nightfall.

Maggie was sitting in state behind the counter when Martin came in. It was a clean, well-kept pub with fresh sawdust on the floor and a big fire in an open fireplace. She had only two customers. Mickey MacGowan, editor of the *Ballycastle Courier* and his chief reporter, Murty Griffin. MacGowan was about sixty and had lost his job as a sub-editor on the *Irish Press* in Dublin for altering a report of an election meeting addressed by Éamon de Valera, at which he had been present. The reporter had written, as was customary, that there were thousands present but the proprietors were astounded to read next morning that only an apathetic handful attended.

'It's me or you, my good man,' said the editor to him the following day, 'and as you're a bachelor you'd better start moving.'

He was a talented man but in recent times sought refuge in sarcasm and derisive anecdotage. Still one could see a certain nobility in his blue-veined face. He was seated on a high stool drinking whiskey and berating de Valera. It was a strong Fine Gael house, for an uncle of Maggie's was killed in the Civil War, on the Treaty side, and another in Spain with General O'Duffy. Pictures of both uncles, Arthur Griffith, Michael Collins, Kevin O'Higgins and General O'Duffy hung on the walls. Party leaders always visited her when they came to town for she was generous with subscriptions to election funds.

Murty Griffin was in his usual Thursday night, closing-time condition: full to the gills with pints of porter. He stood with feet splayed, swaying slowly from side to side and his hands supporting his weight against the counter. He was almost overflowing.

'Go out to the yard, sweetheart,' said Maggie quietly.

'Stick your fingers down your gullet and up with the lot. I'll give you a drop of gin then to settle your stomach.'

Rattling noises came from Griffin's gullet and he turned two raddled and watery eyes on Martin. He growled a salutation that seemed to contain a lot of obscenities and resumed his slow swaying from side to side.

'You're welcome, Martin,' said Maggie. 'We're churning as you can see! What'll you have? A half-one?'

Martin said yes, as it was near closing-time. He was about to apologise to MacGowan for being late and for not having written a line when Griffin took off down the long passage to the yard, hitting off the walls and retching loudly.

'How many thousand times has he committed gluttony?' asked his editor. 'If there is any sort of after-life his punishment isn't hard to imagine. You haven't written anything, Melody? Wasn't it a good job that I foresaw that and did it myself like the Little Red Hen. "I have the whole lot in my head", he said, "Maggie. Just to shove it down on paper." Well I wrote it myself and loaded it with all the venom I was forbidden to inject into this week's leading article. I'll stand the drink, Maggie!'

'Don't be too hard on him,' said Maggie. 'How many times did you fail yourself?'

From the yard came loud cries of anguish as Murty implored the blessed and the damned to come to his aid. Regular customers didn't pay the slightest attention to these performances but strangers who passed by when Murty was 'discharging cargo', as Maggie put it, were often badly frightened. The clock struck ten, Maggie drew the blinds and asked Martin to close the front door. She turned off all the lights except the little one over the till. Martin and the editor finished their drinks and Martin called Maggie aside and slipped her four pounds.

'We're clear now, Maggie, and thank you very much indeed.'

'I'll let you out now and then lock up. I'll let that misfortune out through the kitchen when he has sorted out his guts.'

As they left Martin felt Maggie's hand dip into his jacket pocket. They said goodnight and walked across the little market square in front of the Cathedral. Martin put his hand in his jacket pocket and felt two pound notes.

The editor was denouncing the people who owned his paper.

'I told the Board of Directors they couldn't be poachers and game-keepers and that it would be far better to ignore the event than to come down on both sides of the fence, "O then welcome it . . . a qualified welcome. We must say that it will take the gun out of politics. But we will also have to say that Emmet must wait for his epitaph". . . .'

The editor stood at the street corner and roared, 'Fuck Emmet and his fucking epitaph', which caused three wards-maids from the hospital, who were passing by, to scatter and run away shrieking, 'Did ye hear him? Mother of Jasus, did ye hear the fucker's filthy tongue?'

'Why should I stay in this foul town? I could leave . . . I could still leave . . . but I won't leave. Listen to me, Martin. Follow your own course and don't let life spancel you.'

It was a tune familiar to Martin and to anyone else who came on Mickey MacGowan at the end of a long day. They went up Middle Street and turned down the hill towards the docks.

'And that's the sort of leading article we'll have on Saturday?'

'Oh, Christ no! We emphasised the need for unity and the chairman said we would have to stress community co-operation. His wife is mixed up in this charity ball to raise money for these evicted families up in Sickeen. "Here we have in microcosm the Ireland of the future with Catholics, Protestants and Presbyterians . . ." and all that shite forever and ever, Amen. And do you know the truth of the matter? These two families owe thirteen pounds arrears. Right? There are about thirty people on the committee. Right? Simple mathematics . . . about seven and sixpence a head. They would make arseless dogs shite, the whole

32

fucking lot of them. Will you come with me to the Knight's Club, I'll get you in?'

'Thanks, but I am expected in the Lobster Pot. I'll see you on Saturday and I'm truly sorry about the other matter.'

But the editor was wallowing in a trough of despondency and self-pity.

'What misfortune led me to this awful place. My mind and my soul are manacled! I will drink whiskey with the merchant princes of the town and listen to their pathetic conversation. But at least I won't have to suffer the company of their disgusting womenfolk. Women are strictly forbidden.'

He turned to Martin. 'If you feel the need of a drink tomorrow, if you wish to commemorate your Saviour's death in my company . . . two long rings and one short one and then ask for me . . . but please don't bring along your nasty pimply friend. God speed you!'

Martin was about to turn down Hake Street when the pangs of hunger hit him and he remembered he had eaten nothing since midday when Mrs Anderson had given him lunch: two potatoes, a spoonful of tinned peas and a pigmy whiting. He turned another corner and went down a narrow lane which contained eight slum dwellings, a pawn-office, two fish shops and a crubeen-house which was open from eight at night until one in the morning.

The crubeen-house was owned by two ancient sisters, Mona and Maura. The narrow front room was divided by a greasy counter. Behind it, on a coal range, three pots were always on the boil; two containing crubeens (pigs' feet) and the other rabbits. The old hags sat on either side of the range dishing out the grub. It was an exceedingly filthy place. The floor was covered with gobbets of fat, grease, little bones and strips of pig's skin. Very few of the customers were sober and fights were frequent. Mona was the more agile of the two and she was in charge of the defences: an old harpoon which she kept stuck in the bars of the range so that it was always red hot. If the rows threatened to spill over the counter or if the cleanliness of the food or the accuracy of the change was questioned, Mona caught the harpoon and waved it over the heads of the customers. This had an immediate effect on even the most demented. The year the war ended a Spanish freighter came into Ballycastle to take on a cargo of seed potatoes: the first big ship to call for nearly six years. Some of the crew were given poteen instead of whiskey in some sleezy dive and one of them hit Maura on the head with a canister of salt because of the slow service. Before Maura hit the floor with her skull split, Mona had sliced part of his ear off the Spaniard with the harpoon. That was the only occasion when the smell of roasting human flesh mingled with the other strange smell so familiar to those who frequented the alleyway.

When Martin shoved his way to the counter he found Mona having an argument with a tall, gaunt man in a tattered black top-coat with a rope around his waist.

'I'll give you the feed all right but you'll have to wait and clean the place up. That's the bargain. We're closing down at midnight because of the day that's in it tomorrow'.

The tattered man cursed under his breath and sat on a bench by the wall alongside a huge German who was trying to devour a piece of stewed rabbit out of his hand. Martin got three pigs' feet on an old Army plate, stolen from the local barracks, and sat on the bench opposite them. The man in the black top-coat was looking around inquisitively. He was lean and red-faced and his little eyes darted from face to face around the room. Martin avoided his glances for he knew who he was. He was known as Nature and he lived in a yacht that had been abandoned by an officer in the RAF the day after Britain went to war with Germany. This, however, was not the reason for the nickname but his way of scrounging drink and money. He specialised in collecting genealogical information about strangers in pubs and later approaching them with the salutation, 'Aren't you one of the ———'s from ———? Well, I can tell you that I have great nature for your people,

34

so I have.' A lot of people swore at him and told him to get going, but others gave him money or stood him a drink. Martin knew he was baiting a hook for himself so he concentrated his attentions on the greasy pigs' feet.

The big German was dressed in heavy underclothes, sea-boots and a knitted cap. His face was smeared with greasy slime and rabbit stew flowed down his chest. An ex-U-Boat skipper, he had taken a boatload of refugees from Germany to Argentina, or so they thought. But having got his hands on the passage-money he put into Scotland with supposed engine-trouble, deserted his passengers and made off with the boat. When he arrived in Ballycastle with his lone crew-man he was chartered by the MacAndrew brothers who, on the strength of this piece of post-war flotsam, added a fish-store to their chain of assorted shops.

The German was talking furiously to himself. He spoke hardly any English but now and again he shouted, angrily and inaccurately, 'KO? KO?' Some thought his conscience bothered him, because of the stranded refugees, but he stood over six feet and weighed seventeen stone so even the most curious gave him a wide berth.

Martin left the crubeen-house and headed for the docks. He felt happier in himself than at any time since morning and intended to stay in that condition . . . at least until the following morning.

FRIDAY
15
APRIL
1949

1

Nature cursed and damned the two hags in the crubeen-house for not reminding him that it was already one o'clock on Good Friday morning. He crossed Hake Street and headed towards the dock. May your shrouds not pass your navels, he said to himself, but amn't I as bad myself with all the talk that was going on all day about Easter and this new Republic? He kept going at a brisk trot until he reached the top of the street that ended at the docks and the Lobster Pot. When this street was wet, as it now was, and glistened under the street lights it was difficult to tell road from water when the tide was high. This caused people who only glanced once, when they glanced at all, to walk, cycle or drive in.

Nature had very vivid memories of the last car that went in for it very nearly crashed through the side of the boat where he was sleeping. The crash, the splash and the last lunatic screeches of the passengers woke him. May you not surface, you pack of fuckers, that was a close shave, were his first thoughts as he scrambled up on deck. The car lights were still on and bubbles came bursting to the surface. Not a soul was to be seen but lights began to appear in the upper windows of houses around the dock. The car lights vanished. Doors opened and voices whispered fearfully from house to house. Nature, who could only swim like a stone, lashed the headrope twice around his wrist and lowered himself over the side and down to his shoulders in the water. He ducked his head under water once, raised himself quickly and began to bellow loudly for help. When the rescuing crowds arrived their first task was to heave Nature on to the dock-side and pump the foul water which he had so carefully swallowed, out of his body. The fact that it was accompanied by a large quantity of raw porter was never mentioned, if it was even noticed. But Nature's heroism caused far more talk than the fate of the three young men whose bodies were taken from the dock some eight hours later. His fame was aided by the reluctance of the local paper or public representatives to draw attention to the fact that the crane failed three times before the car was raised or to the long delay before the diver was found and sent down to make fast the cables. There wasn't any public discussion either about the hazards of the place or the fear that caused the trapped men to tear each other savagely before they finally smothered. It was very useful for many reasons to have a hero, even one so unlikely that nobody knew where he came from and no more than three people in the town knew his proper name.

His own accounts of the rescue attempt were not carried in the local paper either but were exported to the Irish editions of the English Sunday newspapers and it was some consolation for the bereaved to read that Nature, as he dived to the bottom, heard voices reciting the Act of Contrition in unison. A limited consolation, perhaps, to those who knew the deceased well (two Madden brothers from Knockbrack and their cousin home from England) and would clearly understand that they were far more likely to have blinded one another with blasphemous blame with their last gasps. But if these thoughts occurred to anyone they were not expressed nor did anyone ask too many questions about where the men were coming from or where they got the poteen which they still reeked of, even after an eight-hour immersion in the dock.

As Nature now studied the dark and unwelcoming face of the Lobster Pot he reflected on the fickleness of life. May you rot with the spotted cholera, he said to himself but he wasn't now too sure who to blame for being outside the pub at such a disastrous time. During his short reign as a hero he rarely touched porter except to quench the fires kindled by lashings of hot whiskey. Not surprisingly he caught a bad cold after the wetting, although the St Vincent de Paul Society and the minister's wife gave him a heap of old clothes and a heavy black overcoat. A collection was also arranged to restore the three pound notes and the ten shilling note which he had on his person when he dived and which had, naturally, melted. There wasn't much collected around the dock but the charitable women did well further up the town. He nearly fainted when he heard Mrs Manning, who was in charge of the committee, promise to lodge all the money in the post office savings bank so that he could only draw two pounds a week. He recovered quickly enough to spin Mrs Manning a fantastic rigmarole: that he owed a few pounds and that this was his chance to clear his conscience and that, by the same token, he might as well buy a bit of a grave and leave a few pounds with Munchie Roche, in the Lobster Pot, to slap a habit on him and make sure he was brought to church and that a smattering of prayers were said and (when he thought the old whore wasn't softening as quickly as he thought she would) that the old lungs weren't improved by the diving and that . . . saving her presence . . . he sometimes passed blood when he relieved himself and that the doctor once told him. . . . She parted with the money and Nature spent it all in a week.

When he was again completely barred from the pubs that admitted him during his heroic period (apart from the Lobster Pot) the guards met him one morning as he ventured up on deck with instructions to go directly to the Courthouse where he would be presented with a mark of respect from the Government. But for the fact that he knew Guard Sullivan well he might have suspected that this was a trick to get him out of the boat and into the County Home as his enemy the Tailor had predicted a thousand times. He trusted Guard Sullivan who promised him on his word of honour that District Justice O'Donoghue had nothing worse than a Government decoration in store for him. He put on his black overcoat and with great satisfaction walked with the guards through the streets of Ballycastle chatting amiably to them and with the people thinking . . . but his satisfaction was short-lived.

A bitch of a medal and a piece of parchment which he couldn't read because it was in Gaelic written in the English script! He didn't even have the satisfaction of wiping his arse with it, the Tailor rejoiced, for the corners were so sharp they would easily open him from arse-hole to scrotum. Well fuck the lousy Tailor, he now thought to himself, for he was sure his enemy was sitting smugly in the pub while he was locked out.

But getting in was only half the problem for he didn't have the price of a drink. The day of the decoration, when Nature's behaviour outraged the very liberal code of the Lobster Pot, Munchie Roche imposed new sanctions. Nature was thrown out two full hours before the official closing-time with clear orders from Roche, his wife and his daughter Nancy, never to cross the threshold again. It took a week's hard bargaining to get him back. He convinced Roche, through the good offices of his soft-hearted daughter, that he was going to head for the County Home as soon as he had said a last farewell to his boon companions from his days of glory. He was careful to mention the name of the journalist, Murty Griffin, who had written the fine things about him which were read by thousands in foreign parts.

Nancy understood, as well as Nature did, that it would be bad for family and pub to have stories written about a man who had recited the Act of Contrition under water (the current version of the story) being hounded into the County Home because of a squabble over a drink. She told her father that while nobody would believe Nature's stories the Lobster Pot would be the loser in the end. When she mentioned her own interest in Murty Griffin to her mother she gained a willing ally for her mother was worried by some of the students who were frequenting the bar recently, particularly a pimply-faced fellow called Billy O'Grady. She overheard the Tailor saying that any girl seen in the company of one of the O'Grady's of Park would be known forever after as a ride.

Nature made his own devious way back but Munchie had the last word. Nature would be allowed in provided he came with the price of one drink, at least, in his pocket and if any further disputes arose he would be barred for good. The pact had held good but now Nature was locked out with only the price of the third of a glass of porter — if such a measure existed — in his pocket.

The single sullen stroke of the half-hour rolled over the town from the clock-tower. 'Bugger you all,' said Nature loudly but only the blind pub-front heard him. But at that moment he heard the sound of voices coming from the far side of the dock. He froze. After a few seconds he heard a voice that sounded weak and muffled followed by another, loud and clear, calling out, 'Throw it up, you fool, throw it up!'

By the living Jesus, said Nature to himself, people! He turned away from the Lobster Pot and headed towards the voices like a dog scenting prey.

He hadn't gone very far when he again heard the weak voice, a voice he knew very well, pleading, 'O Pateen, auld stock, get me up out of here! Don't leave me here, Pateen, my decent man!'

Nature laughed savagely, tightening the rope around his middle and trotting towards the voices that were now beginning to echo off the tall buildings that surrounded the dock on three sides. So the poxy little Tailor wasn't in the Lobster Pot after all! For some reason that Nature would soon find out he was trapped in the German trawler, unable to get out.

The Tailor O'Brien lived alone in a little two-roomed

cottage on the sea-shore near the docks. His limbs were stunted from birth and he had lost the use of one leg. He made his way about on crutches and it was commonly acknowledged that he had the filthiest tongue in Bally-castle. Only Nature and an Army cook called Matthew O'Malley dared take him on in a slanging match. But the Tailor wasn't slanging at the moment. He was pleading piteously for assistance from the depths of the dock.

Nature started to roar laughing as he came to where the trawler was moored. A very large man stood there shouting to the Tailor to throw him up a rope that had fallen from his hand. The Tailor was sprawled on the deck below poking about for the rope with a crutch. He was on the verge of tears.

'Hello there, little Tailor of the lice! Are the fish biting? I always heard it said that a tailor would never be found in flotsam but there we are. . . .'

'The curse of Christ on you, you tramp,' said the big man. 'Come here and give me a hand to get this misfortune out of the boat.'

'He can stay there till the barnacles eat him,' said Nature. 'I didn't get him in there.' He glanced sneakily at the big man. 'Now, if you could get me into the Lobster Pot . . .'

'May you never see the face of God or His Blessed Mother you pox-box!' The Tailor couldn't contain his venom when he heard Nature cashing in on his misfortune.

'. . . and a half-sovereign from the louse-farmer. That's my last word — in Irish or in English! What have you to say now bollocks O'Brien of the slack prick?'

'Shut up for the love of Jesus,' said the big man. 'You'll wake the town. You'll get your half-sovereign and we'll all get into the Lobster Pot but first get this devil out of the boat.'

An upstairs window opened on the far side of the dock and a man's angry voice shouted: 'Stop that noise or I'll call the police! Have you no regard for decent people who want a night's sleep!'

'Sweet Jesus have mercy, it's Macken the councillor,'

41

said the big man under his breath. But before he could do anything about it Nature let a roar across the dock: 'Get back to bed and give your missus a few darts. It's a long time since you troubled her, I hear! Tomorrow's a holiday!'

'I'll put you in the County Home you mangy bundle of rags,' shrieked Macken. 'You're a danger to public health!'

'Well you can say that again, sir! I can smell him down here!'

Nature went to the edge of the quay and shouted viciously at the Tailor, 'Where was the tinker-woman's hand when Mickey the Corner opened the snug door?'

Angry voices echoed back and forth across the dock demanding peace and quiet and threatening the police. The big man caught Nature by the throat, shook him and swore he would pitch him down on top of the Tailor if he raised his voice again. In the same breath he warned the Tailor that he would remain aboard until daylight if he uttered a word apart from his prayers from that moment. The big man was furious for he knew he was to blame for the mishap. His name was Pateen Griffy and he was mate of the *Schlossberg*, the trawler on which the Tailor was trapped. He came from an island off the south coast and was very difficult to understand as he spat out whole sentences as single words. When he was drunk and angry, as he was at the moment, he was almost unintelligible. His brother at home was getting married at Easter and as he found it impossible to get a ready-made suit to fit him he was dealing with the Tailor O'Brien.

The Tailor had delivered the finished suit abroad the trawler at about ten o'clock. When they found that one of the sleeves was too long the Tailor set about fixing it on the spot. The Mate was so pleased to get the suit (for the Tailor had been on a terrible binge for a week) that he produced a bottle of Spanish brandy which he had bought from a skipper who had been arrested for fishing within the limits. When the suit was repaired and the bottle empty the pair came up on deck and were almost shocked into sobriety to find the boat aground against the dock

42

wall. The dock-gateman had abandoned his post and to make matters worse it was a spring tide. With a rope clamped in his teeth the Mate clambered up a safety-chain but when he asked the Tailor to take the slack around his waist he grabbed so anxiously that he carried the rope out of the mate's hand.

The Mate and Nature now squatted on their hunkers and looked down at the Tailor who lay with his limbs askew like a frog that had been squashed by a car. After a moment's thought the Mate rose.

'It's safer to slap him in a sling and hoist him up with the block and tackle. I'll put a line around his middle and you'll haul him in when I have him hoisted.'

When he repeated this for the third time Nature said he understood and would oblige. The Mate caught the safety-chain and slid down into the boat. Despite his size and bulk he was as light on his feet as a dancer and in a few minutes he had rigged the block and tackle and thrown a line to Nature. The Tailor, meanwhile, whined and whimpered and kept asking the Mate what he was about. The Mate remained silent but when the gear was ready he caught the Tailor, trussed him like a chicken for roasting, stuck the hook through the knots at the small of his back and began to hoist him rapidly in the air. The Tailor opened his mouth to scream but no sound came out. He was suspended between the masts with a drowning man's grip on his crutches, swaying and spinning in the dark. The loud rattle of the block brought the people who thought they were rid of the noise-makers back to windows again. The Tailor was hoisted to the limit between the masts still dumb from shock.

'Pull him to you,' shouted the Mate. 'Pull him in and I'll let go slack.'

'What's that you said?' roared Nature. 'I can't hear a damn word you're saying!'

'God rot you, you bad bastard! Pull him to you, I say!'

Nature pulled the Tailor towards the quay wall but as soon as the Mate slackened he also slackened and the

Tailor shot off again into the darkness spinning furiously like a spider at the end of his thread. This second shock brought his voice back and he began to scream in a most piteous way. The Mate flew into a rage.

'You've gone too far this time, you shithouse! Put the cripple's curse on him, Tailor, you son of a bitch!'

Nature responded immediately: 'Wait a minute now, comrade, up a bit now! Right now! That's it! Slack a bit! All right! Slack another bit! Now we're right! Sure we were only trick-acting!'

And he dropped the Tailor accurately face down in a pool of mud on the dockside. The Tailor stopped screaming and began to tear at the knots that bound him.

The Mate came nimbly up the chain, freed the Tailor, put him on his feet and slapped the crutches under his armpits. The poor man was covered in mud from the dockside and tar from the deck and was still quivering with fright. Nature stood sheepishly looking at him. People were shouting further threats from the three sides of the dock. The Mate hit Nature a blow in the chest that put him sitting on his backside in the mud.

'Only I've no time I'd drown you in the dock, you prize fucker! Get up out of that and hurry to the Lobster Pot before the guards come. Come on you too, and stop shaking; you're on dry land now.'

The three of them made off around the dock towards the Lobster Pot: the Mate striding, Nature trotting with his head stuck out in front of him and the tiny Tailor between them swinging creakily on his crutches.

2

As the clock struck two Munchie Roche put down a pint he was filling and announced to a packed house: 'It's time to lift the drawbridge, lads! Out the back with some strong man!' The bar and the little room that opened off it were jammed with noisy drinkers and the air thick with blue-grey smoke. An iron stove with a roaring fire stood in the middle of the floor and the sweat rolled off those who couldn't get away from it. As soon as Munchie spoke Billy O'Grady put down his drink, slipped quickly down the passage that led from the bar to the kitchen.

Nancy Roche was sitting on a chair in front of the fire toasting a slice of bread on a fork. She turned her head lazily towards Billy and smiled at him. The tip of her tongue flicked over her thick lips and she stretched back in the chair. Billy stood and his cold little eyes roamed lecherously over her body: the soft wide mouth, the heavy breasts hanging free in a knitted jersey, the ample thighs. Christ, what an almighty bang! Neither of them spoke. Billy went out the back door and down the yard to where a ladder stood against the wall. He climbed the ladder and pulled up a second ladder which was standing against the wall outside. He placed the two ladders in a corner of the yard and went back to the kitchen. No one could now enter the Lobster Pot and anyone who wanted to leave had to get permission from Munchie Roche.

Nancy was now standing at the kitchen table buttering her toast. Billy came up behind her, put his hands over her breasts and pressed his groin into the cleft of her buttocks. Billy favoured the direct method and although this earned him many a slap in the face he also, as he was fond of pointing out, got an occasional ride as well. Nancy shoved her bottom against him gently, loosened his grip on her bosom and said: 'Down to the shop with you, Billy. You may look in the window but keep your hands of the fruit!'

'Some fruit too, by Jesus!'

'Boldy! Boldy! Take care would Murty hear you. He's very jealous, you know!'

'He's out there pissed drunk. No more than another I'd say he won't rise again till Sunday!' Billy chuckled lewdly.

'I was at confessions yesterday,' said Nancy devoutly. 'Be off with you now.'

Billy went down to the bar where both Roche and his wife were beginning to notice the length of his absence.

45

The Tailor noticed this and said to the man next to him: 'Watch herself there! She thinks your man is groping the daughter. She'll attack the kitchen any minute!'

'And hasn't she reason to be worried,' said the man. 'Did you ever hear tell of a male Grady from Park who wouldn't get up on a cracked plate?'

Billy edged back to his place at the counter where Martin Melody, the Mate, Nature and Murty Griffin were drinking together. He whispered to Martin, 'Your true-love's uncle is in the back room shooting Red Indians off the wall for all he's worth.'

Martin, who was getting groggy, sighed and indicated what he would like Frank Ryan to do to himself. Nuala's uncle Frank was never sober after two o'clock in the day for the last twenty years; apart from spells in Mount Mellary and Roscrea where his family dispatched him occasionally, in the hope of a permanent cure. Martin knew Billy had said this to annoy him. It was one of his latest tricks and Martin didn't like it at all.

'I'm sick and tired of this bloody new Republic that's being announced on Monday,' said Munchie. 'Is anybody here able to tell me what it's all about at all? What the hell difference will it make? What good is it going to do the poor man?'

Since Nature was certainly the poorest person in the company he thought fit to comment.

'Sweet fuck all!' he said simply.

Mrs Roche raised her eyebrows and glanced at her husband. She very rarely spoke a word.

'Language, please!' said Munchie. 'But I see what you mean and I agree with you. But tell me you, newspaperman, why is the man who's responsible for all this nonsense over in America instead of being here at home? Your man with the French accent . . . MacBride. I saw his picture in the *Irish Press*, himself and a few hundred poor devils of emigrants from Leitrim, on the tender below in Cobh.'

A remarkable change had come over Murty Griffin since

Martin had met him in Maggie Fleming's. Having spent the earlier part of the day dulling his senses with porter he was now sobering up on gin. He was reputed to be the least principled and most devious journalist in the provinces and his ultimate ambition was to get a permanent job with one of the English Sunday papers to which he supplied sensational and often baseless stories. Another such story was beginning to germinate in his mind at the moment but he answered Roche's question.

'They want to take the gun out of politics and pull a fast one on de Valera.' That's what you wanted to hear, you bloody thick, he said to himself and turned his thoughts again to creative news.

'They'd want to get up mighty early to pull a fast one on Dev,' said the Mate. 'By God, that'll be the day!'

'I met a man at home last Christmas,' said Martin, 'an old man who lives on the mountain. He was in our shop buying a few things and he said to me, "You there that got college education, tell me why is de Valera knocking around with this fancy widow-woman lately? It's a shocking thing for him at this hour of his life and the good lady he has at home." "What's this, Mike?" I said. "Didn't I hear it on the radio in the Master's house", he said, "that the Taoiseach and Mrs Costello were at some big dinner in London." '

Everyone laughed and Roche laughed louder and longer than anyone else. He came from out the country and had sold his farm to buy the pub. He was a stout man who wore a peak cap at all times, indoors and out, and constantly chewed dried seagrass which he kept in a bag under the counter, hence his nickname. A martyr to insomnia, it was the main reason for his curious hours of business. During the day, if the weather was fine, he sat on a chair near the dock and dozed but he rarely went to bed. Some people said his guilty conscience had come between him and natural rest because (if there was any class of a God at all) the curses of the women, whose menfolk were locked in the Lobster Pot all night, must have fallen on him.

But Munchie didn't seem troubled. He took pleasure out of inciting his customers to the brink of violence and shepherding them back again. Earlier in the night he had to physically separate the Mate, the Tailor, Nature and Pat Power, the dock-gatesman. The Tailor was refusing point blank to give Nature the promised ten shillings. At the same moment the Mate wanted to beat up Pat Power for having forgotten to shut the dock-gates. Power was so drunk that he fell in a heap on the floor as soon as he rose to defend himself and was now propped up beside the Tailor in the quietest corner of the bar.

During the commotion Nature got an opportunity to collar Martin and tell him that he had recognised him earlier in the crubeen-house but didn't want to make free. He asked, gently and fondly, for his father and Martin gave him two half-crowns. It seemed to him now that Nature was a fine, interesting fellow and indeed that the bar was full of interesting and amusing people. He also understood that there was a direct connection between his present outlook on life and the amount of drink he had consumed since evening.

Billy was telling a story about Bishop Mullin's mother, a widow who lived near his home place. The story concerned a bulling cow and the bull's owner who was in a hurry to catch last Mass. The Bishop's mother argued that the cow couldn't have been properly bulled as the bull's hindlegs never left the ground when he jumped and she wanted a second jump for the price of the first. Martin had heard the story before but the crowd were laughing uproariously. Munchie said it would be very interesting to hear what kind of sermon the Bishop would preach at the Mass for the new Republic on Monday. The Government parties and Fianna Fáil would be in church, although Fianna Fáil was boycotting all other official ceremonies. Martin noticed Billy gazing sideways at Murty Griffin, trying to figure out, undoubtedly, how one so miserable in appearance had managed to lay claim to Nancy Roche's luscious flesh. Billy had a high opinion of his own looks, despite his pimples and his lack of height. He was very sure of himself and Martin envied him.

They had been in boarding school together but as Billy was four years his senior there was hardly any contact between them. There was also bad blood between their families. When Father Brendan was a prefect, during his last year, he gave Billy, who was in his first, a terrible hiding and his father complained to the President of St Peter's.

The O'Gradys came from Park, a small village about twenty miles from Martin's home. They had a good farm and a huge, rambling house which they acquired from the fleeing local landlord during the Civil War. Old O'Grady also acquired a public house licence in some remote part of Ireland. When war broke out they turned the place into a hotel. O'Grady had three sons, by his lawful wife, a small pious woman who rarely left the house. It was said that he had various other children scattered throughout the county, for he was given to rampages during which he drank and gambled and pleasured those wives whose husbands had gone to England to seek work. Unlike most fathers, O'Grady was very open with his children about his debauchery and when they reached adolescence took them along on his drinking bouts.

But when the first American troops arrived in Northern Ireland some sort of Holy Ghost descended on O'Grady. He stopped drinking and carousing and began to make money, hand over fist. Two of his brothers were in the US Air Force and in a short time the Park House Hotel was packed every weekend with American officers on leave. The eldest son, Peter, was sent off around the country buying tea, sugar, whiskey and other rationed goods, on the black market. Even when Billy was still in primary school he was often sent along with him as a kind of insurance policy against total drunkenness and debauchery. As a result of this Billy had first-hand experience of the seven deadly sins long before he finished his catechism. The hotel was well staffed with young women recruited, it was said, for their good looks and loose morals. Scandal

49

often threatened but O'Grady, who had abandoned all other vices for financial trickery, was able to ward it off with discreet sums of money. Billy wasn't long in St Peter's when he was christened the White Puck Goat, because of his wispy blond hair and the stories of gamey girls which he never tired of telling.

Martin's mother and brother were forever warning him against having anything to do with Billy. In boarding school the four-year difference in age saw to that and Billy, who behaved like a man in schoolboy's uniform, took little part in school activities apart from the discipline of study, classroom, refectory and dormitory. He regained his freedom in the University and especially in the crazy carousings of Ballycastle. But events at home took a turn that affected his life greatly. His brother, Peter, had gone to America where he became an airline pilot but his younger brother, Joe, had the misfortune to cohabit, drunkenly and carelessly, with one of the waitresses and make her pregnant. When Old O'Grady was told of this he tried the tricks that had worked so well in the past. But this girl's family were numerous and vicious and also saw their chance. They threatened law and disorder if the couple didn't marry immediately. Old O'Grady threw them both out, after their secret marriage, and went back on the bottle with a vengeance. Shortly after his wife died, almost apologetically, and he lost his reason completely.

After a bad beating in a Dublin whore-house he was taken to hospital and shortly afterwards to a private asylum where he remained completely incurable. Joe and his wife returned home but Peter came back from America and with the assistance of Billy and a sharp lawyer, wove a web of law around the property. There was no will made and Old O'Grady would never again be sane enough to make one. Joe was a complete fool and his wife a slattern. The business declined rapidly and they were the real losers. Peter came home frequently and took Billy on tremendous cross-country binges. They were creaming off two-thirds of the running profits for drinking purposes while the lawyers prepared to sell and divide three ways. Billy was doing Arts but had so far passed only one examination and that at the third attempt. Since the beginning of the previous term Martin and himself had become boon companions.

'Give him a dig,' said a voice close to his ear and Martin was jerked back into the company. Billy was smiling his sly, narrow smile.

'He's in love,' he said, with what seemed to Martin to be an excessive sarcasm. Martin realised he was now getting very drunk.

'Did you hear,' said Munchie Roche, 'that Larry de Lacy is home from the States? The Tailor says he saw him up at the Square today.'

'I didn't,' said Martin. 'Are you sure?'

'As sure as God's above,' said the Tailor. 'May I never leave this spot if I didn't!'

Larry de Lacy was his father's closest comrade in arms during the War of Independence and the Civil War that followed it but Martin had heard more about his exploits from other people than he had from his father. De Lacy had gone to America before the Civil War ended, due to a sudden fit of depression, it was said, and never returned. The news of his appearance in Ballycastle surprised Martin and gave the crowded pub another topic for debate. The Tailor and the dock-gatesman (who had somehow regained his senses) began to argue about the big ambush in Bally-laughan, in which Martin's father and Larry de Lacy took part. Billy remained silent. Old O'Grady was a member of the Royal Irish Constabulary before he married into Park House. But Murty Griffin smelt loot and he spoke earnestly to Nature.

'Is it true that you are an Old IRA man and that you fought in Ballylaughan that day?'

The Tailor let out a screech of fiendish laughter and addressed the company: 'Is it him? An IRA man, by Jesus! Sure the pigs wouldn't have him in their army if they had an army! IRA my arsehole!'

'He'd be taken ahead of you anyway, you dirty-mouthed

dwarf,' said the Mate, who was getting rapidly tired of the Tailor now that his wedding-suit was finished. 'Speak up, Nature, and don't mind these fools who would laugh at a fly's fart!'

Nature looked shrewdly at Murty, caught him by the lapels and shouted brazenly at him, 'Not a fucking word without two pounds! Two pound or damn the whisper you'll ever hear!'

'What name should we call you, by right?' said Martin.

'Thomas MacDermott is my name, sonny, but this land-shark made a fortune out of me before and devil the penny I ever got barrin' the odd pint.'

'Now! Now!' said Munchie Roche, remembering unpleasant events. 'Down to the kitchen with the two of you and do whatever talking needs to be done. Off with you now!'

'There was a man called MacDermott in the Ballylaughan ambush. I often heard my father say he never found out what became of him.'

This statement of Martin's caused much surprise but out of respect for his father's name no one, not even Nature, said a word. Only Billy glanced at him in amazement. Murty took his drink in one hand and with the other propelled Nature ahead of him down the passage to the kitchen.

Hours later, as Martin and himself were making their unsteady way home, Billy returned to the subject.

'There'll be trouble about that lie you told about Nature. What in God's name is wrong with you at all lately? One minute you're fine then — Bang — you're off!'

'Go and fuck yourself!' said Martin, as deliberately as he could. 'The next time you start off about love and the drunken side of the Ryan family to me — look out for yourself.'

They stood silently for some time as they relieved themselves against the statue of some forgotten friar from the previous century that stood at the end of Stella Maris Road. Martin was very unsteady on his feet.

'There's damn all wrong with you that a good ride wouldn't cure,' said Billy solemnly. 'I hope you don't mind me telling you but that prissy little virgin up in Monivea will be the death of you. And I wouldn't mind but I know a lovely bit of stuff. . . .'

'I'm not interested in your cast-off cunt . . .' and Martin lurched off unsteadily towards Mrs Anderson's.

'I don't care,' said Billy. 'I've made my own arrangements for tomorrow. She's not all that hot in looks but she has a bottle of whiskey, and a room of her own and she's mad for the magic wand!'

He shook his penis at the stone friar and followed Martin. They had made their way quietly to the top of the stairs when Billy again referred to Martin's enforced chastity. Martin swung at him in the darkness, they scuffled and fell in a heap on the landing. But despite the load of drink, they both realised that it was no time to draw down the wrath of Mrs Anderson and they crawled quietly into bed.

3

'In the name of God, boys, are you trying to bring the curse of the Almighty down on my house? Get up! For God's sake get up quick! It's gone one o'clock. Get up and show some respect for the Passion, the Divine Thirst and the Crucifixion.'

Mrs Anderson was hammering on the bedroom door. After morning devotions, the stations of the cross, a visit to the cemetery and a session of scandalmongering in her sister's house, she returned to find her lodgers in bed snoring like a pair of porpoises. Never would it be said on Stella Maris Road that Mrs Anderson's students slept through the hour of the Blessed Passion! She put the tin of salmon and the tin of baked beans on the table and told the children to prepare the lodgers' dinner. She raced up stairs and began to belabour the door. Billy was half-awake.

'The first station, the scourging at the pillow,' he said. 'Leave us alone! All right! All right! ALL RIGHT!' Martin was now fully awake but his tongue was so thick with slime that he couldn't utter a sound.

'Billy, Billy, Billy! I won't leave this spot until you get up. What about my young family? What kind of example is this on the day Our Blessed Saviour gave His most precious blood to redeem us?'

'Blood! Christ Almighty would she ever give over,' said Martin to himself. He rose on his elbow and clearing his mouth and throat shouted to her: 'OK! OK Mrs Anderson! We're getting up.' A sudden cramp in the back of his calf caused him to turn suddenly and fall out on the floor.

'O, the Lord bless us and save us, they're still drunk! O, look down on poor widows! Get up and get out this minute!'

'All right but for God's sake stop roaring.' Billy jumped out of bed and collided with Martin who was knocked flat on his back.

'O, Mrs Anderson, Martin's Easter lily has sprouted. It's a miracle without a doubt!'

'Shut up you fool and don't make her worse. We'll be right down, Mrs Anderson. Have mercy on the sore heads of the world!'

They put on their clothes slowly, groaning with the pangs of craw-sickness, and went down to the dining-room. Mrs Anderson sat at the head of the table, her elbow propping up her chin wearing what her lodgers called her 'Mother of Dolours face'. One of the daughters came in from the kitchen and put two plates in front of them: a spoonful of tinned salmon and two spoonfuls of beans each. Mrs Anderson poured the tea. She ostentatiously pushed the sugar and milk away from her end of the table. As an additional penance for Holy Week she was drinking black, unsweetened tea. Nobody spoke for what seemed like an age. Martin looked at his plate and was seized with a nervous desire to laugh.

What did the little pink lump and the red mess beside

it remind him of? Who was it said, 'Are you going to eat that or have you already eaten it?' He was about to explode when Mrs Anderson sighed deeply. There was silence in the kitchen as the children gathered behind the door to listen.

'Mary, Anthony, Eileen and Paul! Upstairs! Wash and dress quickly. We're leaving the house at a quarter to two sharp for the Holy Hour in the Dominicans! Hurry now!'

Four pairs of feet dragged disappointedly from kitchen to stairs. They would miss the fun. Mrs Anderson placed her two elbows on the table, clasped her hands under her chin and began.

'You got home this morning?'

Martin's eyes met Billy's. This idiotic start boded no good at all. They fixed their eyes on their plates.

'Do you remember everything that happened after you came into my house last night? Do you realise that . . . that not even tinkers . . . not even the communists would behave like that? O, God help me this day!'

Mrs Anderson began to wail. Big tears streamed from her watery eyes and down her yellow cheeks. Martin was seized with panic. Was it possible that the White Puck Goat had tried to get up on her in a drunken sleepwalk or worse still, had he strayed into the daughter's room? But Billy showed no signs of worry. He was looking straight at Mrs Anderson with a faint smile on his thin lips and no smile in his eyes.

After a few minutes Mrs Anderson composed herself, got up, took a brown paper bag from a drawer and poured the contents suddenly and from a height on to the table. The severed head of the Sacred Heart hopped once and landed in Billy's crotch. He jumped to his feet in amazement clutching himself with both hands. Martin gave vent to his relief with roars of laughter. It seemed that during their early morning scuffles they had knocked over and smashed the statue of the Sacred Heart that stood sentinel over the widow's house from its perch at the top of the stairs. Mrs Anderson blew up.

'I'm giving you your walking-papers now, you pair of low scuts! Be gone out of this house by six o'clock on Sunday. I'm a Christian woman and I'll give you that much notice. You must clear the accounts . . . every last penny . . . or I'll keep your belongings . . . such as they are! When you finish your food go upstairs and pack your bags but nothing goes out that door until I get every penny you owe me into my hand. I know full well where you are kept drinking until four o'clock in the morning . . . and on Good Friday too . . . and the riff-raff that kept you company.'

Martin thought it better to say something.

'We'll buy you a new statue, Mrs Anderson. . . .' She waved a hand to silence him.

'All I want is the money you legally owe me. I couldn't take anything else . . . not a statue anyway . . . it wouldn't be lucky.'

Billy asked her casually how much the statue had cost. This question halted Mrs Anderson in full flight. She screwed up her face and screamed: 'It was a present from Father Alphonsus! It was his wedding present to us!'

You thundering bitch, said Billy to himself, you're out for blood all right. The poorest monk in the most impoverished order wouldn't give such a hideous piece of plaster to an enemy much less to friends whom he had joined in wedlock! Martin got up and spoke as hypocritically as he could.

'We couldn't possibly leave the house without making some sort of restitution. Look, we'll start packing now and at dinner-time tomorrow we'll settle the matter. I'll have a word with Father Brendan about the best place to buy a good statue.' Mrs Anderson calmed down but she didn't say a word.

'You're calling on the priesteen for assistance very often these days,' said Billy as they set about packing. 'Is he going to pay the digs money as well?'

'Somebody will have to pay it. I'm down to about fifteen pounds and there are a couple of other little things to be cleared up. I'm meeting him on Sunday after the match. I promised him I'd go home.'

'Home! But if you go home will they let you come back here again? Have you made up your mind at last?'

It pleased Martin to hear a note of worry in Billy's voice for although their relationship was sometimes uneasy he admired him for his independence, although he realised it was a rather purposeless independence. He regretted his own inability to come to a decision or to speak his mind fully and truly on matters of importance.

'I hope I didn't annoy you too much last night. I shouldn't poke my nose into your affairs . . . but that one really . . . never mind . . . we'll leave it at that. If you do go home it will be the end of the good times we had.'

'Forget about last night, Billy! I was pretty drunk myself, a lot drunker than I realised at the time. But tell me something. Who is this girl you mentioned . . . cut out the pretence now, you remember it well . . . you weren't that much under the weather.'

Billy smiled his private smile. Then he looked serious.

'Fair enough so. She asked me twice to tell you to call into the Four Masters Hotel for a drink. Stella Walsh is her name . . . and before we go any farther let me tell this much. I was never with her. I tried often enough but somehow or other. . . .' Billy laughed drily and pulled a face at the memory of defeat. 'But I'd say you'd be all right. She had a long run with Wally Watson before he got married and he wouldn't waste a second night with anyone who wouldn't let him exercise the lizard, as he says. Here! In honour of the feast and the new Republic I'll divide my fortune with you.' Billy threw a handful of French letters on to Martin's bed, where he was packing his suitcase.

'I got them cheap from the dock-gatesman last night when he was pissed. He buys them from the crew of the Liverpool boat. Take them and do her in remembrance of me! I'm off to make contact with my own little Easter bunny. She told me to call when the family are out at devotions. She has a room in a little house at the bottom of the garden and there's room for me at her bottom. Tooraloo! I'll see you tomorrow.'

When he was gone Martin put the unfamiliar objects in his fob pocket and resumed packing. Sooner or later he would have to face Nuala and the quarrel which would undoubtedly follow. He could hear Mrs Anderson scolding the children.

'Hurry up now for the love of God. It's gone two o'clock. We want to get a good seat near the altar. Hurry, I say.'

Martin finished packing as quickly as he could.

4

Martin spent the rest of the day until nightfall rambling by the seashore west of Golden Strand. He was trying hard to decide what to say to Nuala that night and to his brother on Sunday. But to no avail. The harder he tried the more his thoughts strayed into the past. Since he was told of Larry de Lacy's homecoming, after twenty-seven years, he knew in his heart as well as his mind that his father was truly on his death-bed. The thought was in his mind for some time but as the doctors still talked of an operation he hadn't extinguished a slight ray of hope. In a way this was one of his reasons for not visiting the hospital for two months. Hoping for good news and the joyful occasion which this would bring about: hoping that this would lift the darkness from his mind and let him feel at ease in the presence of his father. He now realised that it was but a childish dream and a feeble defence against his shyness and loneliness. He tried to keep them at bay as best he could. But his mind was crowded with problems he couldn't face and this merely deepened his depression.

He made another attempt to concentrate his thoughts on the most immediate of his problems, but his mind was more practised in evasion than in concentration. Better take them one by one and see what courses were open to him. He suddenly remembered with shame how he had gone unprepared to meet his brother the previous day and how pathetically weak his behaviour had been. But some facts were crystal clear. His state scholarship, and the independence it gave him, was at an end. Gone also was his academic status and Ballycastle was too tight a town to allow his other activities the secrecy he would have wished for. Even if his mother allowed him to come back for another term, in defiance of his brother's scheming, his attendance at lectures was so bad that he would scarcely be allowed to sit for his examinations without the kind of good will he had clearly now exhausted. But did he really want to continue? He couldn't really say or perhaps he didn't really care, one way or another.

His mind shied away from the unpleasant subject and indicated that it might be as well to deal with the girl first. He changed his course and headed for the high hill behind Ballycastle where the professional and business classes of the town lived in large houses surrounded by trees. Nuala Ryan's father owned a flour mill and her mother's family owned the biggest garage in the town. She was an only child and as the marriage had long since ceased to be a union her presence alone gave some meaning to her parents' life together and kept them under one roof. It was her unhappy home life, which resembled his own in many ways, that first tied their knots of friendship. As time went on they found increasing pleasure in each other's company, comforting one another and looking forward to the time when they would be equipped to live the happy life they would spend together. When the weather was fine they cycled out in the country and spent hours discussing their future; a future free from the mistakes which had blighted both their families.

Nuala always maintained that it was Martin who changed and that this had ruined their relationship. She blamed simple things in a simple way: that he had begun to drink, that he took up with Billy O'Grady and other undesirables, that he lost interest in his studies and, in particular, that he was leading both of them into sin with his increasing preoccupation with her body. Martin started at the memory of her sudden cry of fear as they stopped on the brink of complete union: fear of her own body's frantic response to the desire which Martin had awakened. She broke away from him and thanked God aloud for her deliverance. But she didn't blame Martin unduly and this endeared her even more to him. Later, when she confessed to her favourite Jesuit, in whose counsel she had such blind faith, things changed more rapidly.

When his sister Mary was sent away from home in disgrace because she was found to be having a child for her lover, he confided in Nuala and sought comfort in his anger and loneliness. Mary was the other half of himself. He thought Nuala welcomed the opportunity to bind him in a mesh woven by herself with the aid of her mother and the Catholic Church. After this they drifted further apart. His visits to her house became more infrequent and she was at Mrs Anderson's door as often as her pride allowed. But although he had spent most of his time since the previous summer in Billy's company he hadn't sought the company of another girl. Nuala still had a hold on him which he didn't fully understand and although he was far from happy with their relationship he wasn't sufficiently unhappy to bring it to an end. Nuala was terribly suspicious of any female seen in his company, particularly what she called 'common girls of the town'. She excused her suspicions by blaming a series of casual affairs for her mother's estrangement from her father but in another way it betrayed the influence of her affluent family background.

The square two-storey house, set well back from the road, was surrounded by tall trees and neat flower-beds. It was a fine solid house without ostentation and sometimes, in his troubled state, Martin regretted the lack of courage which prevented him from making his own pact with the devil and with Ballycastle and hanging his hat in Monivea. He took more pleasure out of this particular fantasy than any of the others he entertained for he knew it was truly unrelated to fact and therefore free from any of the bitterness of reality.

Nuala opened the door before he rang the bell. She put her fingers to her lips and whispered: 'Shhh! Mammy has a bad headache and she's lying down!' Martin heard a door bang somewhere at the bottom of the dark passage that led to the back of the house. He realised that his arrival had interrupted yet another row between Dick Ryan and his wife. They went into the sitting-room where a log fire blazed. Nuala sat on a chair near the couch. This is going to be a serious talk, he thought, all bodily contact is strictly forbidden.

And as always happened, even after their long relationship, he was again acutely aware of Nuala's beauty and understood why he wasn't really attracted to other girls. It was generally acknowledged that she was one of the most striking girls in Ballycastle. She wore her dark hair shoulder length and it framed her fair unblemished skin and grey eyes. But her body was her most striking attribute, particularly her long slim legs which seemed to stem from a point closer to her shoulders than her hips. Martin took pleasure out of watching people turn in the street to stare after her swaying hips and shapely legs. He was also proud of the fact that he alone knew the secret of her seat of love which lay slumbering at their junction. His mind jerked again: 'I am sorry! I beg your pardon but I was thinking of something. . . .'

'I said we don't have much time. I don't want to keep you too long because Mammy will need me soon. We better be straight about this. Did you do the things I asked you to do on Tuesday?'

Tuesday! He pretended to be preoccupied but what the hell had he been asked to do? He had it! Without a second thought he launched into yet another instant decision.

'I'm going to confession tomorrow evening in the Franciscans. We can meet for a cup of coffee afterwards and have a long chat about things. I'm not meeting my brother until Sunday evening. I'm going home. It's the best thing to do. It's what I have decided.'

He cringed with shame as he saw her face light up with genuine pleasure. She ran across the room to him, mewling with delight and kissed him quickly. But when he tried to pull her down beside him on the couch she glided away, pretending not to notice.

'O, Mattie, I'm so happy. Everything will turn out right now. He said everything would work well for us if we were straight with each other and with God. My prayers have been answered.'

Here we go again in the blather and nonsense stakes, he thought, and a fine bloody quagmire you have landed yourself in this time with your lies. Nuala kept babbling on happily.

'I was so upset when I met Uncle Frank today . . . if you only saw the state he was in . . . and he told me the two of you were in the Lobster Pot. I started to write a note to you breaking the whole thing off and then Mammy and Daddy started an argument about what I should do next year . . . and about you, of course . . . and I felt so miserable and so lonely.'

Martin got terribly uncomfortable as soon as she hinted that he was partly responsible for her parents' latest resumption of hostilities. She had a way of letting things like that slip, by way of no harm, and he suspected her motives. But he had successfully weathered another storm. Billy had recently said their joint motto should be, 'Never do today what can be put off till tomorrow.'

'You're right, Nuala,' he said. 'I had better go and have an early night tonight.' She seemed annoyed that he reacted so promptly to her earlier suggestion but with a shrug of her shoulders she walked with him to the front door and again asked him not to speak loudly. Voices rumbled indistinctly in the depths of the house. Could it be, thought Martin suddenly, that Dick Ryan has taken leave of his discretion and brought home the big sulky-looking cashier from the mill whom he is knocking off at the moment? But the thought fled when Nuala put her arms around him and kissed him gently and chastely on the corner of the mouth. He shuddered with desire as he felt her breasts full and heavy against his chest, but as he moved to embrace her she again slipped from his grasp.

'What time in the café? Shh! Don't make a sound. Eight will be fine. I'll be waiting for you.'

How the hell will it all end, he asked himself, as he walked down the hill towards the town. Well, he had seen her at any rate and tomorrow was another day. Then he remembered the invitation to drink in the Knight's Club, but as he was making his way there he changed his mind suddenly and without a second thought walked into a public 'phone-box and put a call through to the hospital where his father was. He had to wait some time for a connection but when he had put in the money he heard a familiar voice, Sister Kevin, a nun from his own home parish. He was very fond of her because of her compassionate nature, particularly for the helpless and poor, and also because she never called his brother anything but the 'Holy Father', because of his pomposity and self-importance.

'Well, well, Martin,' she said warmly. 'How well you knew when to ring. We were just talking about you here. Do you know that your Dad is having the operation tomorrow? He is indeed. The surgeon is coming down from Dublin. We'll have Big Martin on his feet again in no time, just wait till you see.'

The warmth of her welcome and the fact that she never referred to his eight-week absence from any contact with his father touched Martin unexpectedly and tears filled his eyes.

'And your father's old friend has been here since morning. The greatest scoundrel in the Irish Republican Army.'

She cried out suddenly in mock horror, 'Stop that now Larry de Lacy! Mind would the nurses see you!' A cool voice with a strong American twang came on the line.

'I remember your fine round thighs, Maggie Walsh, long before you covered them up with that silly habit! Hello there, young Martin. Larry de Lacy here. How's tricks with you? Listen! A driver and a car will be at the Corner Bar

63

tomorrow. OK? Tomorrow at twelve sharp. OK? Be there and you'll be taken here, pronto. Driver's name is Coffey. He hasn't a lot to say for himself but he is one hundred per cent OK. Your Dad is fine. The spirits are high. I'll look forward to meeting you. Seems a bit odd talking like this when I've never seen you. Cheerio now, son. . . . Oh, by the way, I met His Holiness your brother Brendan just now. . . .'

At that moment the operator said time up and broke the connection. Martin felt strangely calm and contented and the tears had dried on his cheeks. The voice from what seemed like mythology had given him courage. He walked briskly home and stole quietly upstairs to bed.

SATURDAY

16

APRIL
1949

1

The town of Ballycastle was completely transformed on Saturdays. Its streets and shops were taken over by the people of the surrounding countryside. They filled the little square in front of the cathedral with masses of potatoes, vegetables, eggs and poultry which they sold to the townspeople. Travelling salesmen also set up shop there and their hardware and delph glistened on the footpaths. The little square filled with noise and vitality: people struggled against the milling throng, bargaining and arguing with the country people, complaining about their avarice and obduracy. The market was the first commercial activity of the day and from there the crowds flowed through the centre of town on a day-long shopping spree.

The *Ballycastle Courier* was published on Saturday and from early morning small boys with piercing voices hawked it through the streets and pubs. As the day went on the network of narrow streets in the centre of town became crammed with people, as the businessmen of Ballycastle battened on its hinterland. Those who came to sell at the market returned home with a load of goods. As the crowds swelled travelling musicians came to play and collect money on street corners and the centre of town was filled with the sounds of music and the babble of excited voices.

Large raw-boned women came tearing out of shops, clutching shopping-bags and gaggles of children, to pass the time of day with neighbours on the other side of the street, oblivious to traffic. Horns hooted angrily, bicycle bells rang, brakes screeched and carters cracked their whips and cursed.

Apart from visiting the market the people of Ballycastle didn't usually shop on Saturdays but because of the general close-down on Good Friday, Easter Saturday was an exception. This meant that streets and shops were packed with an almost solid mass of people. So also were the pubs as those who had abstained for Lent began to slake their seven-week thirst. The churches were also busy. A lot of country people preferred to go to confession to strange priests from the orders to fulfil their Easter Duty: priests who wouldn't recognise peculiarities of speech or personal patterns of sin: the sins peculiar to country folk such as writing malicious and anonymous letters, calumny, the casting of spells and those secret sins known only to rural bachelors and spinsters. The women, laden with shopping-bags and children, crowded into the churches and the air was full of signs and groans of relief as they gasped and muttered through their penances. Small boys stood in porches and against church railings, minding barrels, laths, chunks of newly-sawn timber, corrugated iron and all sorts of farm implements as their fathers repaired their souls within.

There were three classes of sin, however, which only Bishop Mullin himself had the power to absolve: the distilling of illicit spirit, poteen, perjury; and attendance at non-Catholic services. Nobody knew how long it was since anyone had whispered the third class of reserved sin into the Bishop's ear but he kept it on the books to ensure the continuing purity of the true faith in his diocese.

Although most of the business classes of Ballycastle were of country stock and some of them no more than a generation removed from the hobnailed boots, as the saying had it, they nevertheless regarded this Saturday hosting as a kind of invasion by strange tribes. This was also the attitude of the ordinary townspeople, even the people of Irishtown. All in all, the townspeople regarded themselves as being more refined and sophisticated in appearance, speech and behaviour, than these crude people who could be heard where they couldn't be seen. The cornerboys, who were plentiful in the town, came to watch the passing show from vantage-points in doorways and from the parapets of bridges, nudging and winking and imitating accents and strange phrases. They were careful, however, to pitch their voices with a certain discretion.

Towards evening the soldiers came out of the barracks on leave and paraded in twos, accompanied by servant girls and wardsmaids from the hospital, from the Square to Irishtown Bridge and back again, chattering and laughing loudly at very private jokes and making plans for the night and the weekend. Saturday was indeed a special day.

Some businesses did better than others, however. Saturday's throng put very little into Maggie Fleming's pocket and if she had to depend on them for a great part of her living (which she didn't) she would scarcely prosper. Politics were responsible for this state of affairs. Most of the country people in the vicinity of Ballycastle were either followers of de Valera's party or supporters of the IRA. And ever since the unfortunate apparition at Berrysfort, Maggie was regarded with disfavour by the people of that area. Strong farmers, who had been Blueshirt supporters, and country shopkeepers whose customers had deserted them for the day, came to visit her and drink moderately. Maggie looked on Saturday as a rest-day which she could enjoy at leisure. At eleven o'clock when Martin breezed in with a message for Billy, only Councillor Macken and Mattie MacHugh, the District Court Clerk and Secretary of the Brothers Pearse Hurling Club, were there ahead of him. Martin had slept well and he greeted the company cheerfully. Maggie and her daughter Sal were behind the bar.

As soon as Martin opened his eyes that morning he noticed Billy's bed hadn't been slept in. A good time was had by all he said to himself: Mrs Anderson didn't speak at all, when she placed the boiled egg in front of him, but sighed deeply. Her personal Lent didn't come to an end until after the last Mass on Easter Sunday. He was anxious to see Billy later in the day and Maggie was by far the most reliable person to deliver a message. But before he could open his mouth Mattie MacHugh had hooked him. Sunday's big match for the Republican Cup was Mattie's sole topic of conversation for weeks and so far that morning he lacked an appreciative audience.

Councillor Macken sat on a high stool reading the leading article in the *Courier*. He was the leader of the Fine Gael party in the town council and as Fianna Fáil were boycotting Monday's ceremonies, apart from the High Mass, it was his duty to lead the parade and unveil the memorial on the Square afterwards. This was the pinnacle of his career in politics and he was cultivating a habit of not responding too readily to remarks from any Tom, Dick and Harry. Martin reminded him of the unpleasantness early on Friday morning so he just lowered his paper slightly and grunted. Mattie was already in full spate about the match.

'Give him a medium of porter, Maggie,' he said. 'Wait till I tell you! Did you read the paper yet? Did you see the team we've picked? Do you know what the Canon's done? You won't believe it I guarantee you! I own to God I hardly believed it myself when he told me!'

'Give the boy a chance, for God's sake,' said Maggie, with a ringing laugh. 'Take it easy, Mattie, little love. Sure, mightn't he even go a pint?'

'O, fill whatever he wants! A pint it is! What would you say if I told you that the Canon has picked his nephew P. P. . . . Patrick Pearse . . . his sister's son . . . for tomorrow's match . . . what would you say to that?'

'Isn't that the skinny little pale-faced lad who got his place on the county minors last year and was taken off at half-time?' Martin didn't like Mattie very much, for when the Canon was present he was afraid to open his mouth at all.

'Never mind that now! Never mind last year. What would you say, though, if I told you that the lad is picked to play full-forward — marking the Kipeen Burke!'

That was the morning's trump card without a doubt. Maggie stopped filling. The Councillor put down his paper. Martin shook his head from side to side in disbelief. Sal began to titter and scratch her breasts with excitement.

'Full-forward indeed! Sure the Kipeen'll kill him!' Sal had no regard for the ritualistic politics of the establishment. Mattie winked at Martin, paid for the pint and took off again.

'Isn't that just what I said to the Canon!' "Two terms in Maynooth, Canon!" I said. "Sure he's not even half-way through his growth. His bones are soft! For the love of God." But there are no flies on the Canon. Do you know what he said to me? "Matthew," he said. "Whoever tries to kill my nephew will have to catch him first and who's going to catch him? A boy who won the hundred yards and the two-twenty in the provincial championship. The Kipeen Burke would as easily jump over the moon as he would catch up with Patrick Pearse MacCarthy. It's all decided. He'll play between the middle of the field and the twenty-one yard line and the Kipeen Burke and the other savages from Bawnmore will regret the day they set out to bring my Republican Cup into disrepute." That's what he said, upon my solemn oath!' said MacHugh, as if he were afraid that some of the Canon's sentiments might be attributed to him.

'I hope the little creature minds himself,' said Maggie with feeling. 'That Burke article should be in a cage above in the Zoo far away from civilised people, instead of being allowed to play games and put decent creatures in hospital.'

'Tell me this,' asked Martin. 'Why did Bawnmore enter a competition they haven't a chance of winning . . . ? Not a snowball's chance in hell have they got. Isn't that why you're going to have a full house up there tomorrow?'

'If we knew that we'd be all right,' said MacHugh gloomily. 'They have no chance, as you say, and you know what their delegate . . . that foxy-haired Shanahan fella . . . said at the County Board meeting. . . about the Cup. . . . Well, we'll not bother repeating it in front of the women,' he said unctuously.

The Councillor put aside his paper. It seemed to him that all this talk about a hurling match was lowering the dignity of the new Republic and therefore his dignity. He pointed a finger accusingly at the paper.

'This bloody country is in a right mess, in a bloody mess, I tell you. I've just finished reading that leading article . . . wait till I see that alcoholic editor! Even our own paper, that stands firmly behind the policies of our party, even this paper has to drag in this nonsense about Emmet's epitaph. "Emmet will have to wait." What the bloody hell, savin' your presence, has Emmet got to do with it? Are we to give this new republic a fair chance or are we not? Are we going to give a fair chance to peace and put an end . . . an end for all time . . . to guns and gunmen in politics? That's all we want. And with all due respect to the Canon, I greatly doubt that this cup of his is any great help to the cause if it means getting involved with these anti-Christs from Bawnmore. They're not fools either, more's the pity!'

'Ah, well now,' said Mattie MacHugh, 'you'd have got any odds you asked for against Bawnmore getting as far as the final. They were to meet Killenamanagh in the semi-final and Killenamanagh went to extra time against us in the County Final last year before Seaneen Fahy got the winning point for us. How did it happen that half the team didn't turn up for that semi-final and Bawnmore had to be given a walk-over? There was a story put out about sugar in the petrol-tanks of the cars but not even a child would believe that.'

But Councillor Macken had a bellyfull of hurling at this stage.

'To hell with it for a story! All I'm saying is that the memorial up at the Square is the most important thing . . . apart from the official declaration, that is, and the whole ideal and what the Government, the Taoiseach and even

70

that bloody ex-gunman who repented, Sean MacBride. . . .
Where there's shame there's grace, as the old people said,
and the same can't be said about that Spanish bastard who
was born on the high seas. . . . Éamon de Va–bloody–lera.
. . . That's all I'm saying. . . .'

Martin swallowed the last of his pint, told Maggie not to
forget to tell Billy he wanted to see him and to give Mattie
a pint and that he'd pay her later and good day to them all
and to the Councillor too and he was gone out the door.

The Councillor snorted contemptuously. As the Mate
was fond of saying, he was running before a fair wind now
with all his reefs out.

'And why does that young cornerboy have to come in
here, I ask you, except of course to bum drink and fill his
bag with stories so that he can imitate us all again in the
Corner Bar and the Lobster Pot?'

'Leave him be,' said Maggie. 'He's a nice young lad and
he has his own troubles.'

'I hear the father is bad and that the other murdering
gunman Larry de Lacy has come home from America to
bury him. May the eternal fires of hell stay hot for both of
them. They shot your uncle, Maggie! The law of the gun
was their law, but by Christ we bested them and with the
help of God we'll see them down too!'

'That young lad shot nobody,' said Maggie. 'Would you
leave it now like a good man!' There was an uneasy silence
with Mattie MacHugh wriggling on his seat and pretending
to be somewhere else when Salamander made one of her
rare contributions to the conversation.

'He's very nice so he is and I wouldn't mind having a
feel off him at all but he's going out steady with that one
with the long legs from above in Monivea.'

'Go down to the kitchen, my love,' said her mother
gently, 'and put down the kettle. A drop of tea will do us
all good.'

Mattie MacHugh decided it was time to steer the conversation towards less dangerous topics. 'I heard you had
a bit of trouble yourself the other night with a gang of

latchicoes. Good Friday too above all the days in the year!'

'Did you hear that? Well let me tell you that you'll hear more about it too. I'll see to it that that filthy, diseased, public menace they call Nature is carted off to the County Home and that the Tailor is thrown out of his cottage and shifted up to a council house in the new scheme . . . whether he likes it or not. If you heard the kind of language I had to put up with from those two. But I have the power!' And he slapped his hand viciously on the counter.

But Councillor Macken was right about one thing. About three minutes after leaving Maggie's, Martin was sitting in the Corner Bar telling it all to the manager, Michael O'Malley, an army cook. The bar was on the ground floor of a large building on the corner of the Square and Middle Street. The whole building was taken over by the MacAndrew Brothers when they heard a rumour that a big Dublin firm was showing an interest in it. Although they already owned about a third of the town's business these middle-aged and barren brothers spent most of their time on the look-out for outside concerns who might be thinking of setting up in Ballycastle. For about twenty years they had conducted a kind of guerrilla warfare against Woolworths, in the course of which they had acquired a variety of sites and derelict buildings all over the town. But although Michael Thornton was only their manager he did exactly as he pleased in this strange pub. According to the most knowledgeable topers in Ballycastle, it was the only pub in the world where all the mirrors were inside the bar and facing the windows. Visitors who were not familiar with the design of the place were often startled to hear Michael say as he poured a drink with his back to the windows, 'I see Professor Lydon reading the paper down at O'Donnell's corner. It's nice to know the poor devil's still keeping an eye on what's going on in the world.'

They assumed, naturally enough, that not only had Michael got eyes in the back of his head but that he could also see around corners. It was a rather small, dark bar with a lot of little snugs like confessionals along by the walls. These were very useful when business of a private nature was being discussed and women could enjoy a discreet drink during breaks from the rigours of shopping. It was easy to slip in or out of its two side-doors and vanish from sight.

But as well as being a barman Michael ran a large and varied business. In a room, at the back of the shop, he kept an incredible collection of goods that found their way there from a variety of places: army shirts and blankets, hobnailed boots, bottles of Spanish brandy, cans of paint and brushes, ropes for thatching, coils of barbed wire, buckets, ropes and scores of other odds and ends. But Michael had no truck with petty thieves.

Early in his career as a receiver of dubious goods, a girl who was employed in a private nursing home in the town offered a gold watch for sale. Michael did his duty as befitted a respectable citizen. He gave her a carefully marked pound note, as an earnest of good-will and told her to come back for the rest when he had examined the watch. The girl was barely half-way across the Square when Sergeant Lynch came up behind her on his bicycle and took her into custody. Michael was highly praised in Court, got valuable publicity, and petty thieves gave him a wide berth. He was interested only in public property which wouldn't be too diligently pursued and which he could get rid of rapidly. The pub toilet was a great sight on fair days: crammed with big countrymen trying on army shirts, stockings and boots. But Michael was always so easy-going, always ready to spin a yarn or tell a joke, that one would never guess he had so many different and delicate irons in the fire. It was said that only once was his placid surface shattered. Hearing strange noises coming from one of the snugs one day he pounced to find a tinker woman giving hand-comfort to the Tailor for a fee of five shillings which she loudly and aggressively claimed although full satisfaction had clearly not been achieved. The Tailor was strictly barred from the premises from that day to this.

'May he never see the face of God or His Blessed Mother

the dirty little carfartin' bollocks,' said the Cook. 'But I heard Nature gave him one almighty blast of filth when they were hoisting the Tailor out of the boat. The devil mend him! Macken the Changelings' son!'

'Tell us! Tell us, man!' Michael urged gleefully as he wiped the counter his eyes darting in the mirrors. 'We heard you were in the Lobster Pot!'

Martin told his story but found, of course, that his audience knew more than he did himself. Just then there was a loud roar from one of the snugs.

'Come up and take the wheel, Steve! We're coming inside the lighthouse!' The three of them laughed. It was the Mate.

'I barely had the bolt off the door when the big galoot fell in on top of me, new suit and all and as drunk as arse-holes. There wasn't head or tail to be made of him so I gave him one drink and shoved him in there to sleep it off. He's dreaming now the poor hoor, but wait till you see this. . . .' Michael went to the till and took out a thick leather wallet. 'Two hundred and sixty shaggin' pound. Going to his brother's wedding. Now, if it happened in other pubs that we won't mention. . . .'

They all nodded with perfect understanding and then the Cook asked Martin if it was true that his father was having an operation. He said he was waiting for a lift to the hospital and was relieved to be able to say so truthfully at last.

'Wait a bit now! Hold on now, lads!' said Michael, suddenly, his eyes darting at a mirror. 'We'll have a bag of laughs in a minute now. Peggy Shanahan from Knockbrack and the Kipeen Burke's cousin and that other mountain of meat from Berrysfort are after colliding down at the bank. Yes, indeed, they're coming this way. I've a tin can and a galvanized bucket for the Shanahans.'

The three women came in noisily and sat on a long bench at the back of the shop. They ordered two glasses of orange and a half-glass of port wine for the woman Michael had called 'the mountain of meat'. Herself and the Kipeen's cousin were about the same build and were dark brown from working in the fields under wind and sun. The Shanahan woman was red-haired, gaunt and bony and had a habit of poking her head forward when she spoke, like a wicked gander about to launch an attack. The Cook sat happily on a high stool swinging his legs and making small-talk about the weather. When they wanted to stir things up Thornton and himself worked in tandem.

'Well I heard a most amazing story this morning, if it's true,' said Michael, in an offhand way. 'I heard the Canon's sister's young boy was going to mark the Kipeen Burke in the big match tomorrow? That's if it's true at all. Some people never stop putting out false rumours.'

'O, be the Jasus it's true all right!' said the Cook. 'I heard the Canon said when he picked the team that he'd blind the Kipeen with speed . . . or something like that.'

The two big women laughed silently, their huge bodies shaking. 'We'll see who'll be blinded in the end of the day,' said the Kipeen's cousin. Michael threw out fresh bait.

'Well, I think myself . . . and mind you I heard others saying it in this shop already this morning . . . that it's a damnable class of an insult to the Kipeen to send a school-boy in to mark him. Sure if he hits him the least tip it'll be said that he's only fit to beat kids at the end of his days and himself and Bawnmore will be disgraced.' And for a moment there was a glint in the Kipeen's cousin's eye but she glanced at her large companion and they both laughed.

'The whores' melts have a plan all right,' whispered Michael quickly.

'Disgraced and shamed for all times,' said the Cook. 'They'll be making no songs about that kind of carry-on! That should get them,' he whispered to Thornton.

The red-haired Shanahan woman poked her head forward slowly like a weasel cornering a rabbit, her mouth narrowed and her bony hands tightened around her glass of orange. She began to speak quickly but with great deliberation, her eyes fixed on a spot in the distance. The

Cook and Thornton exchanged rapid winks of pleasure. They had provoked her.

'It's not Bawnmore or Bawnbeg or Knockbrack that's disgraced this day, my good men, but Ireland, let me tell you, Ireland and this whore-house of a town that was a disgrace since the first stone was raised here. A town that never rebelled but always opened its gates to the enemy as easily as its womenfolk opened their legs to them after. We know all that and we know it full well. When the country to the east rose up in Easter Week what did the brave people of this town do, those of them who hadn't already slapped on the enemy's uniform? What did they do, my good men? They rose up bravely and attacked a couple of poor Germans who were making clocks and minding their own business. They attacked them so savagely that the Royal Irish Constabulary had to take the creatures into the barracks for safety. O, well and truly do we know and understand who has cause for shame.'

While she was speaking her two companions sat solemnly staring at the floor while the Cook and Thornton wriggled with silent mirth. But Martin found her intensity frightening. Her strength of feeling reminded him of his mother and how she was able to round off her weakest arguments with, 'That's an end of that now! Your mother is tired and there's work to be done.' He also now realised who the woman was. Her two brothers were in the IRA and were interned in the Curragh Concentration Camp during the war. Shortly after their release one of them got a severe bout of pneumonia and died. But as far as the people of the locality were concerned, Peter Shanahan had been murdered by the Irish State as he was in very poor health when he was released.

Thousands attended his funeral and when three strange men fired a volley over his grave the police made a baton-charge through the cemetery in an attempt to arrest them. This was done against the advice of Sergeant Lynch, who took sick leave as soon as he heard Shanahan had been anointed. But the police got the worst of matters, for the local men had hidden their hurley sticks under tomb-stones the previous night and they routed the police out of the cemetery and down the road. Many were hurt during the vicious fighting, including this woman, Peggy Shanahan, whose leg was broken.

After drawing a deep breath she continued her rapid monologue.

'If de Valera fooled us, as he did, who beat the Blue-shirts of Ballycastle for him? Who broke every pane of glass between this corner and the Protestant Church when General O'Duffy boasted that he'd hold a meeting in Bally-castle if he had to march over dead bodies? Who threw the kettle of boiling water over Old Macken the Councillor so that the nurses in the hospital spent the night cutting the shirt out of his flesh with scissors? And tell me, who's being fooled by this circus on Monday and the dances and the Cup and the slab on the Square outside? Let me tell you this, my good men, no tricolours will fly over our vil-lages to celebrate no more than they'll fly over Belfast or Derry or anywhere else in our stolen counties where they're forbidden by law. This is a great republic surely and if de Valera reneged — and he did — what can one say to Costello of the Forty Chins and his lisping lackey with the fake French accent.'

The Cook was in like a flash. 'Bedad then, it isn't long since you were singing another song about Sean MacBride, when he was defending IRA men in court.'

'It's a great pity, indeed, that we can't be as wise before the event as we are permitted to be afterwards. But, my good men, those who remained faithful and true will always have a right to speak. Those who remained true in spite of English jails and Irish jails. . . . Aye, and the Eng-lish hangman brought over by an Irish Government to do their dirty work for them. . . . Those who remained true till death choked them. . . .'

Her emotion now got the better of her and she was sob-bing tearlessly, while her companions tried to calm and soothe her. Thornton and the Cook were embarrassed at the turn things had taken and sought to relieve the tension but before anyone had time to do anything a wizened little man wearing a long black coat and with a peak cap pulled down over his eyes spoke from the back of the shop. He had slipped in unnoticed during Peggy Shanahan's outburst.

'Keep up your courage, Peggy Shanahan, and may the Lord have mercy on the souls of the brave. Don't lose heart! The game isn't over yet and last shots haven't been fired either!'

The red-haired woman turned and looked directly at him and her faded blue eyes were still tearless.

'With the help of God, you're right, Colm Coffey. When good men were easily counted you weren't absent. God bless you!'

'Come with me,' said the little man to Martin. 'We haven't a lot of time. Your father's being opened in two hours' time and the roads are black with traffic. Good day to you all.' He turned abruptly out the door and Martin hurried after him.

'Is that Martin Melody's son from Ballymeara?' asked the red-haired women. 'He seems a nice young lad but he'll hardly be as good a man as his father was in his day. May the good God shepherd him through his troubles this day.'

'He's a decent young fellow,' said Michael. 'I think he's feeling the weight of the world at the moment.'

'The poor creatureen,' said the fat woman from Berrysfort. 'He has a nice little face and lovely blue eyes. You'd love to bring him home and spoil him a biteen.'

The beginning of a lewd smirk flickered over the Cook's face but it quickly vanished and he said, instead of whatever he meant to say, 'Fill them again, Mick . . . give the women what they fancy and may the Lord have mercy on the dead . . . and the dying!'

They all said 'Amen' to that.

2

Martin hadn't travelled far with Colm Coffey when he

realised his pilot was in no mood for small-talk. It was clear from the way he was dressed and how he drove the car that he was re-living a scene from his youth; on a military mission for Captain de Lacy. Civilian affairs were of no interest to him at the moment. Martin was just as pleased for it gave him an opportunity to collect his thoughts and prepare for the ordeal ahead. At all costs he was determined not to upset his father in any way or give him any inkling of the gravity of his condition. He tried to rehearse what he would say, just in case he might let slip a well-meaning but clumsy remark when the time came. His thoughts had strayed miles away, however, when the car stopped with a flourish of gears and brakes at the main door of the hospital. Coffey jumped out and opened the door for Martin, who thought for a moment he was going to salute him.

'You know your way, I suppose?' he said. 'I'll wait here till you're ready to hit the road again.'

Martin went up to the third floor where his father had a private room. When he got to the last flight of stairs he saw Larry de Lacy on the landing, waiting for him. He recognized him immediately from a picture he had seen in a local newspaper years before. While he wasn't a tall man, he looked even smaller because of his very broad shoulders. His legs were curved, like a cowboy's, and when he moved he gave the impression of going sideways as well as forward, rather like a crab. A navy-blue suit accentuated his dark, tanned skin and he wore a black broad-brimmed hat. His eyes were a very pale blue and he had hardly any eyebrows. He stretched out a hand and gripped Martin by the shoulder. His native accent, which was instantly recognisable to Martin, was highlighted by a strong American twang.

'We better be smart,' he said. 'The nurses came in to get him ready, just now. We'll have a long chat later but we mustn't tire him too much now.'

As he was speaking Larry was steering Martin firmly by the elbow to his father's room. The door was open and two nurses fluttered about the bed. His father turned his

79

head slowly towards the door and Martin noticed a flash of apprehension in the sunken eyes. But he smiled warmly and said, 'Good man, Martin! You had it well timed! I've been telling them since the day I came in that the knife was the only job that would put me back on my feet.'

Martin remembered Larry's advice but before he could control himself he began to babble away about how hard he had been studying and exams and college life until he felt Larry's grip tightening on his elbow.

'If I met him in the middle of Texas I'd know where to place that unmistakable stream of old guff!'

The father laughed and then coughed a little and a tremor of discomfort crossed his face. Martin also noticed that the yellowing skin, which had changed his appearance so much for the past three months, was much darker now and that his curly black hair had begun to thin back from his forehead. He also noticed that his father's head now seemed the most substantial part of his body, which barely made an impression on the bed-covers. He noticed these things almost impersonally, as if he were observing a stranger. Larry's firm grip propelled him towards the bed-side and he spoke again.

'We're getting in the way of these women and their work. Look here, old vagabond, good luck to you and God speed the day when the three of us will stand at a bar with glasses in our hands!' Larry placed his large brown hand on the faded one which lay slackly on the bedspread.

When Martin came close to the bed he got a heavy sickly-sweet smell from his father's breath. The pernicious root was in his stomach. He took his father's hand gently and said, 'We won't be far away, Dad! Good luck to you!' And again he noticed the startled flash as his father's eyes caught his directly. Martin thought, so this is what people meant when they saw 'death' in someone's eyes but his father cut across his thoughts.

'Thank you both! The knife's the only hope now. You came when I wanted you most. God bless you and you too Larry. Look after this boy, he's all heart and no sense!'

He tried to press Martin's hand but dropped it and turned his head away. Before he realised he was moving Martin was steered out the door and down the corridor towards the stairs. His body and his mind were now equally numb. He could scarcely comprehend that he had actually seen his father and spoken to him. Larry spoke gently as he moved him forward.

'We'll go down to Sister Kevin now. She has a little office on the ground floor and you can rest there for a while. You've had a bad shock but you were great . . . really great.'

'I'm really all right, Larry. I'm fine now. But there's no chance. There's really no chance. God Almightly, he's wasted away to nothing under the bedclothes!'

He trembled a little and his limbs felt terribly heavy. Sister Kevin came to meet them. She had a bottle of brandy on the table in her room but after making them welcome she vanished discreetly. Martin sat at the table and longed to be on his own.

'This place is quiet and out of people's way. Take it easy for a little while and let it all off your chest. Not a word now. Have a drop of that, nice and easy, and when you feel up to it come down to the Imperial Hotel. I'll be in the bar. Do that and you'll be OK.' A slight pat on the head and he was gone.

Apart from the sudden weariness which he never had experienced before, Martin felt nothing but confusion. His thoughts raced madly and were beyond his control. Memories from the remote and recent past flashed through his mind. He tried to control these racing thoughts and come to terms with the immediate present. Then, quite suddenly, the racing stopped and a childhood memory crowded out all the others.

It was a summer Sunday and he was ten when his father took him to the provincial football final. His older brother had no interest in sport. It was the first time he had a whole day alone with his father and away from home. His father met old friends and comrades at the match and

81

afterwards they all met in a bar. Martin was put sitting on a high stool at the counter and given glasses of orange. It was also his first time in the company of grown men, as they told stories of matches long ago and tales of battles and political meetings and people whom Martin had read about in books. Time flew and when his father tore himself away he remembered that they had had nothing to eat since breakfast.

'It's a day out of time,' he said. 'As we've burned the candle we may as well burn the stump!'

They went to the biggest hotel in the town and although the kitchens were officially closed, Martin Melody had ways of getting around people and they were given a meal, all on their own, in a corner of the empty dining-room. As they ate Martin asked his father about the War of Independence and other things that he had heard discussed in the bar. For about two hours in the dining-room and another hour and a half in the car, as they drove home through the night, his father told him stories about his life as a young man. He told him of how he met Larry de Lacy and of their many adventures together in the Tan War and in the Civil War. He spoke of men who died, who were wounded, who lost their health or emigrated. . . . He vividly recalled his disappointment when they reached home.

A heaviness again filled his chest, as it had filled it that night, when he remembered his mother standing silently in the dark doorway, her hands by her sides and with no expression on her face. He remembered how she caught him and embraced him roughly, saying in a strange voice, 'God protect my darling son! Up to bed with you this minute and not a peep out of you until midday at least. Poor little mite, just beginning to grow!' And when he climbed the stairs with the heaviness rising from his chest to his throat and choking him, his brother met him on the landing and hit him across the face with the back of his hand saying, 'You little pest, you could have asked him to come home and not have your mother worried stiff all night!'

And later, when the tears of anger and disappointment had dried on his cheeks, he came out again to the landing to listen to the tense, muffled voices from below and heard his mother say, 'And keep your meddling hands off my children, Martin Melody. I'm providing for them and I'll rear them and be very clear about that. . . .'

His father said something he couldn't hear but his mother raised her voice as she answered him.

'That's the end of the matter! You can be sure it won't happen again! I'm going to bed now!' And he heard her go to her own room at the other end of the house and a little later heard his father go out, start the car quietly and drive away. Martin went into his sister Mary's room, woke her and before he had time to explain anything he burst out in angry tears again, sobbing.

'Poor Dad did nothing wrong. Nothing at all. We had great fun. I hate her! I hate her!' But Mary understood without being told exactly what happened and she took him to his room and sat with him, soothing him with funny stories, until the sobbing ceased and he fell asleep.

And now again the heaviness rose and dissolved and he put his head on the table and wept as wildly as he ever wept as a child; but now he didn't look for anyone to comfort him.

3

'Your mother disliked me at first sight,' said Larry de Lacy, as they ate a meal later that evening on their way back to Ballycastle. It didn't seem at all strange to Martin to be discussing family affairs so intimately with someone whom he had met for the first time that day. Larry had put him at his ease from the first moment they met and his complete frankness encouraged him.

'It happened that your father and myself were sent to a meeting of the women's section of the movement above in the local hall in Ballymeara. The usual crowd of earnest poor devils, delighted to be in touch with the lads who were off to die for Ireland! Useful in their own way and generous too . . . except in the way that would have made me happy to live a bit longer for Ireland! Then this tall girl came in and sat on her own. She was a stranger to me. Well, it was just like a movie. Your father lost interest in the meeting and kept on looking at her for the rest of the night. Not that she minded that either, quite clearly. It all happened like that!' Larry snapped his long fingers. 'When the meeting was over the two of them walked towards each other and started a serious discussion about politics. Then she said she had to go home and your father had to offer to escort her. It was then I was introduced to her and I told her, by way of a joke as I thought, to be careful as Melody was mighty quick on the draw. Well, she raised her head and bored holes through me with her eyes and without looking away from me said to Martin, "I take it, Mr Melody, that this offensive halfwit is not a close friend of yours. I accept your offer. Thank you!" That's how it started. Two months later they got married. . . . I was best man and I'd almost swear that that was the last time your father got his own way about anything that mattered to him!'

'So all the stories are true? About love at first sight and the romantic wedding and all that . . . ?'

'Sure! But what's so strange about that? Don't those things happen every second day of the week, without war or hysteria or anything?'

Martin thought for a moment. 'I'll tell you why, Larry. Because when I came along there wasn't trace or tidings of love or anything like it; nor had there been for a long time, as far as I could make out!'

'Nothing at all?'

'Nothing at all but close to the opposite. No! That's not true . . . it was nothing definite . . . more like the lack of something.'

'Leave it so, boy! The night is long for talking. We both need this meal. No one is as tough as he likes to think he is. I'm older and more battered by the waves of the world than you are and I know!'

The rich well-cooked food was a welcome change for Martin after two terms of Mrs Anderson's canned cooking. His appetite was sharpened by a long fast and the drink he took to compose himself after he had released his grief. He also noticed that Larry was given to long periods of total silence between animated bursts of conversation. He ate slowly and tried to bring to mind all he knew of his family background.

He was more familiar with his mother's background, for almost all his knowledge came from her. She had a strict rule which prohibited discussions about family affairs with strangers and this meant anyone who didn't actually live under their roof. She often spoke of her father, Maurice Brennan, who reared her after her mother died in childbirth, just a year after their marriage. His deep love for his wife was easily transferred to his daughter. He had an old, established business in Ballymeara, as well as a farm, and he devoted the rest of his life to the temporal and spiritual welfare of his daughter, whose good looks increased with age. She always maintained that her father didn't spoil her, as her father was strict in matters of discipline and very religious. Spoiled she may not have been but she enjoyed power and authority long before she went to board in the most expensive convent school in the province. She discussed the business with her father as she would with a partner. Her father often said that she would be hard put to find a life-mate who could equal her inborn instinct for management. He said this with pride and in fun but his daughter repeated it with bitterness, on the rare occasions when she could be coaxed to talk about the past at all.

But for a time it seemed that a partner would not be required at all. She was always devout, both by inclination and precept, but this was nurtured in boarding school where the regularity of life suited her perfectly. During Christmas holidays, when she was in her last year, she told her father she felt an urge to dedicate her life to God. She hadn't made the final decision and asked her father to pray for her intention and he advised her to pray for guidance. When summer came her mind was made up and she entered the order that had educated her. Her father accepted her decision without question and may even have welcomed it. The First World War was coming to an end and life in Ireland was becoming increasingly unsettled. He had no strong political views and he opted for silence and a quiet life. A year after his daughter entered he sold the farm and the following year decided to sell the business and retire to live in a small hotel near the convent, so that he could visit her regularly. Before he had time to advertise the property his daughter walked in one evening and told him, in the calmest possible way, that she didn't have a true vocation and after numerous discussions with her confessor had decided to return to the world. That was the end of the matter. She had decided.

The following day she took over the business with strict orders to her father to relax and enjoy his old age. This he did but nevertheless he died suddenly the year after her marriage. Martin could well believe that people would be reluctant to question his mother about her reasons for leaving the convent as they would be to ask for her reasons for entering it. It was the will of God. It was also the will of God that Martin Melody came to Ballymeara, helping to organise a revolution, and that they married. On the face of it it seemed a good match from her point of view. He was from the other side of Ireland and it seemed his family had cut him off because of his revolutionary activities. This ensured that they wouldn't be plagued by a meddling mass of relatives. He was a leader of men and strikingly handsome and when peace came they would work together in harmony without interference from anyone.

But her will, in the guise of God's will, didn't work now as it hadn't worked earlier in the religious life. She sometimes said, when her mind was less embittered, that it was the war and what followed the war that created tension and trouble between them: that Martin couldn't settle

86

down, that he had no idea of marital responsibility, not to mention the regular and invariably dull life of a small-town shopkeeper who had no interest in shopkeeping. But when she spoke like this Martin knew she was endeavouring to be charitable and that she really believed her husband's fecklessness and headstrong disobedience were at the root of their troubles. She was convinced there would have been no trouble between them if he had agreed to abide by her decisions and her counsel. But Martin also realised that nobody would now know the full truth of their relationship. Larry de Lacy broke in on his thoughts.

'It's easy to be wise after the event, Martin, but I always got the impression that your father and mother remained strangers for many years after they were married. And when they did get to know each other that they found out something quite dreadful: that they should never have married at all. Brendan and Mary were kids at the time and your father came out to the States to ask for advice, something he never did before. I told him I had no advice to give, that he would have to make up his own mind first and that we could talk then. He didn't like that at all. He walked off without another word and for days I thought it was the end of a friendship. Then, after some days, he rang me and said his mind was made up and that he was going back because of the children but that he needed some way of gaining his own independence. We went into partnership again then, working for this lottery that's illegal on the other side. Things improved for a while, I think . . . but you know the rest yourself or most of it at any rate.'

Yes, said Martin to himself, why wouldn't I! The child of the reconciliation that failed to bud or blossom. It was an unpleasant thought which never before entered his mind. But Larry was now philosophising as he warmed a glass of brandy between his palms.

'Your mother had a great advantage when it came to fighting. She understood the difference between mental domination and physical domination and she had patience. Your father had great physical courage but mental conflict pained and sickened him. He was a very impetuous fighter as well. The night of their meeting in the hall, your mother saw the man who was in command the day the Tans fled in Ballylaughan and being the determined and strong-willed woman she is, she decided to capture him for herself. Of course she was completely wrong. If your father was the wise and far-seeing leader of men she imagined him to be he wouldn't have fought as he did at all that day. In fact his tactics were so opposed to any kind of established military practice that the Tans scared and took off. They must have thought they were up against some diabolically clever plan and opted for discretion instead of valour! If they stood their ground they would have decimated us. We were outnumbered five to one and their firing-power was ten times better. But the gambler's throw won the day!'

The warmth of the brandy spread silkenly through Martin's body as a new understanding illuminated his mind. This brought him both joy and sorrow but he welcomed his increased comprehension.

'Did you ever think of why your mother left the convent . . . her real problem with the religious life?'

'She never said much about it to us . . . or to me, at any rate . . . just that she discovered during a rather severe retreat that she hadn't a real vocation and left. It was one thing I always respected her for . . . it cannot have been an easy thing to do at that time.'

'Indeed it was not. But I still don't think she was fully honest with herself or with any of you when she said that. If the order decided to make her Reverend Mother and put her in complete charge I'd take my oath she'd never have left. No, she was too domineering for a vow of obedience. She couldn't have obeyed a stupid command or indeed any command at all from a person she regarded as stupid. Only the top job would have suited her. Doesn't it make sense?'

'And what about my father? He was far from being a domineering person when I got to know him . . . in so far as I ever got to know him.'

'He was a man cut out by nature for the kind of organisation we had, in this part of the country particularly. He was in command because people loved him and because of the loyalty they were willing to give him. That may have been another of your mother's mistakes. When the Truce came and afterwards the Treaty she expected him to join the Free State Army for a time, so that he could enjoy the official public recognition she felt he deserved. When that was achieved he would return to the business and the bosom of his family. She had it all worked out in a terribly sensible, simple way. . . .'

'It was God's will again,' said Martin with heavy sarcasm as he emptied his glass.

Larry ordered two more brandies and the bill. Night had fallen and Colm Coffey's shadow could be seen through the frosted-glass doors as he stalked up and down the corridor.

'Well whatever about God's will she didn't put your father's will in the scales at all. And she didn't get a real chance either for she didn't see him again until the Civil War was over. The same war was sillier and more sordid in this part of the country than in most other places and everyone was heartily sick of it long before it was over. I cleared off to the States and I don't think your father tried very hard to avoid capture in the end.'

Colm Coffey stuck his head in the door and looked anxiously at Larry. They were heading for Kerry and Colm was itching to be on the road. Larry nodded agreement.

'Look, we'll have to head back to Ballycastle but a few important things must be said. What did your father want from life? Something your mother could never understand and it's important that you should understand it now. At the end of the day he wanted enough to satisfy his rather simple needs . . . that and his personal freedom. No drudgery or dragging or anybody giving him orders. This drove your mother to distraction. He'd be in the shop, during the time he tried hard to fall in with her way of life as best he could. There he'd be and next thing he'd hear music coming from Redmond's pub down the street. . . . Well, I don't have to tell you how that day would end. From what I hear you'd understand easily enough. This is why the job I got him suited him down to the ground. He was on the move, meeting different people and he could go home whenever he wanted to.'

'He was more often away than at home, particularly since Mary left.'

'That's another important matter. He was over on business with me when your mother found out about Mary. Your mother didn't tell him very much in the letter but that she had done what she thought necessary to save Mary's honour. He went back straight away and the next letter I got was from England. He was in a fury and swearing to do time if he didn't find Mary and take her home. You know, of course, that she did a quick bunk out of the discreet home where your mother had lodged her. A week later I got another letter. He'd found her . . . herself and the poor bus conductor and both of them as happy as the day's long!'

Larry laughed and stroked his face with his fingers as he watched Martin's surprise at this new revelation.

'Wait till you hear! He found them in some little flat or room in London. They were both working. You know how a thing sticks in your mind? "I don't stay too long with them," he said in this letter. "They are all the time looking at each other and brushing up against each other and I know very well they don't hear me at all half the time." He was very pleased. They couldn't get married of course. It seems your man's wife was put away years ago and isn't getting any better. At any rate, your father gave them whatever money he had and gave them his word of honour he wouldn't say a word to anybody.'

'He could have told me. He knew very well how close Mary and myself were. I'm really surprised at him.'

'Don't be! There were good reasons. Mary didn't want you to have another bad fight with your mother until you were finished in University. But she was also terrified that her mother and the priest would come to rescue her from sin if they got the slightest clue. And then . . . just think of your father! At long last he had one of his children all to himself and depending on him. But as far as you were concerned it was never intended to keep you in the dark for longer than they thought necessary. Didn't you have enough on your mind without adding to it? Anyway he gave me their address for you last night. . . . Come on now or Coffey will take us out at gunpoint.'

The car was at the door with the engine running. Larry sat in a corner in the back and wrapped himself up in a woollen rug. Martin was prepared for another period of silence so he fixed his eyes on the back of Coffey's head and began to digest his newly-acquired information. Larry straightened up suddenly.

'Jeez, but it's bloody cold! I've spent the last twenty years dodging winter and spring but I'm really caught now. Listen, Martin, we might as well get it all over with before we reach Ballycastle. I'm not telling you what to do. I have given up taking horses to water any more not to mind trying to make them drink! I'll just put a few things to you and then it's up to yourself. A few more drinks and it should be early bed for you . . . and it mightn't be a bad idea to keep an eye on the drinking after tonight. You've put in a hard day, see?'

'I see,' said Martin and he felt disappointed that Larry hadn't suggested some definite course of action to him. 'I'll have to make up my own mind and that I must do to-morrow. But I'm really pleased about Mary and about her and Dad . . . really pleased.'

'Good! Now tell me, where are you going to spend the night? I think you should steer clear of that terrible lodging-house, after what you told me. And as we're on the subject here's some money your father had for you this morning. He gave it to me in case he'd be in the theatre before you arrived.'

As Martin took the envelope he thought, did I ever have more need of it and then he remembered Billy and what he had said about Stella Walsh on Friday. He might as well try his luck. Tonight, above all nights, he could see no reason at all for discretion.

'I'll stay in the Four Masters Hotel. It's in the middle of town and I kind of know a girl who works there.'

'And damn the bit of harm if you do either,' said Larry heartily as he snuggled into his corner and went to sleep immediately. Martin was left to stare at the back of Colm Coffey's head. Things were again taking a different turn from anything he had even half-planned. He thought idly of Nuala and of his promise to go to confession. It was after six now. As the old people had it, it all depended on the turn of the cards. First he would go to the hotel. It was a discreet and secluded place, so secluded indeed that many people in the town had difficulty in finding it after dark. It was half-way down a narrow alleyway, near the Pro-Cathedral, surrounded by derelict and semi-derelict warehouses. It was built by a group of businessmen in the town, as an investment, but was managed by a succession of resident manageresses who gave it a certain reputation for laxity. It was the haunt of customers whose needs created its atmosphere and tone: musicians from dance bands, commercial travellers in their thirties, young army officers and the younger sons of the town's well-to-do families. Drunks and known trouble-makers were strictly forbidden as were most of the town's students. It was Billy's brother, the pilot, who introduced Martin and Billy to the hotel but Martin never returned as it was the only hotel in town which had a reputation for providing accommodating female companionship and news travelled fast in Ballycastle! Stella Walsh, who worked in the bar and who had sent him the message, if Billy could be believed, was known to him only by sight.

Larry woke up as they slowed down on coming into Ballycastle, and just as Martin began to feel drowsy from the movement of the car, the heavy meal and the brandy to which he was not accustomed.

'Here we are,' said Larry, 'and just in case we forget later, I'll see you in this hotel about half past ten on Monday night or else you'll leave a message there for me. You'll have seen your brother and other things will have been seen to. So let's leave it at that. But remember, if it's independence you want, make sure you get the substance and not just the shadow.' He gave Martin a slap on the shoulder and laughed. 'Take note, my young student, of this poor bitch of a country and all this rumpus at the weekend. Isn't that right, Colm?'

'Meaningless shite!' said Coffey, over his shoulder as he parked the car on the Square. The streets were still crowded and sounds of merriment came from the pubs along Middle Street as they walked towards the hotel.

As they were about to turn into the alleyway they were hailed by a tall red-haired man in a trench-coat who was carrying an armful of leaflets. Martin recognised him but before he could tell Larry that he was one of the Shanahans of Knockbrack, Colm Coffey introduced them solemnly. Shanahan pumped Larry's hand.

'A hundred thousand welcomes back to Ireland, Larry de Lacy. It's a great honour for me to shake your hand. It's many the story I heard about you and this laddeen's father, the poor man. It's a bad time you picked to come home. . . . But never mind that now. We're not all fooled, so we're not. Some of us aren't satisfied to stand muttering in the corners. We'll see to it that the shame is lifted from this part of Ireland at any rate. You did your share in your day. We have to fight another battle now!'

Larry spoke respectfully to him about his brother's death. He seemed uneasy in his company.

'He wasn't the only one, much as I miss him. Think of the hundreds and thousands who also died rather than bend. Good luck attend you, now and at all times!' He handed them copies of his leaflet and strode rapidly up the street pressing them into the hands of the passers-by. Martin looked at the leaflet. It had a black border and carried a short message under a big black heading,

THIS 'REPUBLIC' IS A FRAUD

'What is he going to do?' Larry looked at Colm.

'That crowd will always do what they think they have

to do. I don't know what he might have in mind but he will do something as he said it so bluntly.'

Larry shrugged his shoulders and asked Martin abruptly to guide him to the hotel. He was getting more uneasy and when they got there he shoved his way roughly through the crowd at the bar, ignoring the glares and protests of men and women alike. The place was packed, mainly with musicians and their womenfolk who were celebrating the end of the ecclesiastical Lenten ban on dancing. Martin saw Stella Walsh flying up and down behind the bar. She saw him too and stood on tiptoes to wave. This caused some men to turn and stare belligerently at him. Stella never lacked admirers.

Larry got large whiskies for Martin and himself and a bottle of stout for Colm Coffey. Waves of drowsiness swept over Martin in rapid succession and he moved through the crowd to a corner where he found a seat. From then on he was in a state of total confusion. He heard people speaking loudly but could not make any sense of what they were saying. Then he imagined he was walking along a street with great difficulty as he was losing control of his legs. A priest seemed to be shouting at him and wouldn't let him try to explain his difficulties. Suddenly the ground rose towards him and hit him a heavy blow on the shoulder.

Familiar voices surrounded him again and this time he seemed to be in bed and thought he recognised Stella's voice among them. She was telling him to be quiet and rest and that it was wrong of him to shout at priests in church when he was drunk and no matter how hard he tried the words wouldn't come. Then he began to fall rapidly into darkness, tried to pull against it, failed and then his nightmares came to an end.

1

At ten o'clock in the morning Stella Walsh came into the room where Martin was trying to wake up carrying a cup of tea. He found it hard to keep his eyes open, his mouth was coated with a chalk-like slime and his stomach fluttered with spasms of nausea. All that bloody whiskey last night, he thought. He tried to prop himself up on his elbow but a sudden spasm of pain in his head caused him to collapse again, groaning. Stella laughed sympathetically. Three years in the hotel had taught her to respect the pangs of hangover. She put the tea on the bedside table, sat on the bed and placed a cool, dry hand on his forehead.

'You poor fellow! I have some aspirins and tea to wash them down. You can sleep away for another few hours and then you'll be fine. Up now, this won't take a minute!'

She slipped a hand under his head, raised it and put two tablets in his mouth. She then held the tea to his mouth and forced him to swallow it. He felt the bitter pills slide slowly down his throat and his stomach turned again but she forced him to drink it all. Then she settled the pillow under his head and tidied the bedclothes.

'Sleep away now. I'll call you before mid-day and you can attend the drunkards' Mass across the road.'

She patted his forehead and walked to the door. The

blind was drawn and the air heavy with stale whiskey fumes. Martin became aware of this and of his stale body smell and he retched dryly but controlled himself.

'Keep everything down now if you can and if you can't there is a washbasin in the corner. Say nothing! This is one of the special services of the house . . . the only hotel in town that supplies the corporal works of mercy at no extra charge!'

Martin relaxed and felt a surge of sleep come over him. He muttered to be sure and wake him and was almost fast asleep again before she closed the door.

When he woke again he felt a lot better but his head still throbbed and his body felt bruised as if he had played a tough game of football the previous day. Snatches of his nightmare returned and he felt scared. Never before had he suffered loss of memory because of drink. He sat up in bed and began to fire questions at Stella.

'Were you talking to me here last night? What was going on? Please tell me everything immediately.'

She stood between him and the dimmed window with her hands on her hips smiling at him. She let up the blind and let down the top of the window.

'First of all, Martin Melody, would you lie down and stop looking like someone who saw a ghost. Lie down and I'll tell you everything. I shouldn't have teased you last night and the state you were in. There was no damage done. Nobody was beaten, hurt or arrested or anything. Take it easy!'

She sat on a bed on the other side of the room and began to fill in the missing memories of the previous night.

'First of all Larry de Lacy went off . . . you don't remember that? He'll be here tomorrow night around ten. Good! So you remember that much. Well, at some stage or other before he left you strayed out without anyone seeing you and down you went to the Franciscan Church. We're not too sure about what happened after that, but it seems that yourself and one of the priests had a shouting match and he ordered you out of the church. You came back

96

here after that. You told us that a mob attacked you and that you called Bishop Mullin and Cardinal Mindszenty some choice names. At that stage there was no sense to be made out of what you were saying and Larry de Lacy and myself got you up here to bed. And I can tell you that Larry is a gamey one. When we had you in bed he made a grab for me and out of the room I thought I'd never get! But he's really kind and he looked after you well.'

But Martin was barely listening to her. So it wasn't a nightmare at all but snatches of reality. He broke out in a sweat that was caused by fright as much as drink. This was it! This was the last straw!

'This is the end, Stella. What in the name of God will I do now? I'll be run out of the town as well as the college. . . . Holy Christ Almighty!'

He began to thump his head on the pillow as if he hoped to knock these terrible memories out of it.

'Well I'm damn sure the Honourable Nuala Ryan won't approve of this kind of conduct,' said Stella, getting to her feet and imitating Nuala's gait, swinging her hips and speaking very precisely. 'What's this I hear about fighting with a priest in Church? How do you expect one of the Ryans . . . not to mention the well-heeled O'Donnells . . . have anything to do . . . I'm sorry Martin, but that one makes me sick.'

Martin forgot his troubles for a moment and concentrated his thoughts on Stella for the first time. She stood in the middle of the floor with her hands on her hips, as usual. She was bare-legged and wore a white housecoat, the top and bottom buttons of which were open. She didn't seem to be wearing very much under it either. She had come straight from the bath and smelt pleasantly of soap. But she also noticed the change in his attitude and laughed.

'Ah, ha! So last night's whiskey is making its presence felt, is it?'

Martin felt ashamed and a little angry that she was able to read his thoughts so clearly. He wasn't too sure, either, if he really enjoyed the imitation of Nuala.

'Now, now! Let's have no sulks. It's time to get up now. I'll run a bath in the bathroom at the top of the stairs and I'll leave some shaving gear there for you . . . the one we keep for stray swallows . . . and you'll be on the pig's back then. It might be as well for you to miss Mass. I'm not trying to damn your soul or anything like that but it might be a day for discretion, if you know what I mean. And the most important thing of all, when you're finished in the bathroom, ring the hospital . . . or would you like me to ring for you?'

Martin said he would ring himself as they wouldn't be likely to give much information to a stranger. He was rather shocked, after what happened the previous day, that he hadn't already remembered his father's operation. When she left he got up and walked unsteadily to carry out her instructions. When he was dressed he went down stairs and rang the hospital. Sister Kevin came to speak to him and as soon as he heard her voice he knew the news was bad.

'He had a good night, Martin, a very peaceful night. He'll be a bit groggy and sleepy for a while and it might be as well not to come in today . . . not for more than a quick word at any rate.'

She didn't mention the operation at all. He would have to ask her directly. She remained silent for an instant and he heard her draw breath slowly.

'Well, Martin, I'll put it like this. The doctors weren't very encouraged by what they found . . . at first at any rate. But they managed to do quite a bit after all. His heart is very strong, Martin, very strong indeed. He could put up a great battle yet.'

Martin thanked her and put down the telephone. He had the full story now. They opened and they closed again and now one could only wait and hope that the pain wouldn't become unbearable. Of course he had already accepted this possibility but now he knew for certain. And this certainty dispelled a lot of his own personal worries. It was true for Larry de Lacy. He would have to make up his own mind about his future. Stella came out of the dining-room and asked with her eyes. He shook his head.

'It's just as I thought. They opened and closed and are saying very little. I knew yesterday he had no chance.'

'I would like to be able to tell you that I understand how you feel but I can't. My mother and father both died within a month of one another when I was still in the cradle. The aunt who reared my sister and myself was so cruel to us that I really enjoyed listening to the sods falling on her coffin. I know it's a sin for me to feel like this, but I can't help it.'

'The only thing I regret is that I never really knew him and that I never will now but I'm truly fond of him. I suppose that means something too.'

'That's what I believe anyway. Where will you go now? Will you need a bed again tonight or will you go home?'

'Leave my name in the book for the time being. I've a few things to settle before I meet the Holy Father. That'll be all right, I hope. One way or another I'll be back. There's a bill to be paid anyway.'

'The bill is not the most important thing at all. But you carry on and we'll see you later . . . and I hope we will.'

Martin stood at the door of the hotel and looked up and down the alleyway. A crowd stood at the door of the Pro-Cathedral pretending to hear Mass. The sleepy sound of the organ and the atrocious singing of the choir could be heard clearly in the alleyway. He saw Nuala's uncle leaning with his forehead pressed against the cold wall of the church. Every now and then his shoulders quivered. It wasn't difficult to guess what exactly occupied his thoughts and those of his shattered companions — where would they get an illegal cure for their agonies. Martin went down the lane and came out at the lower end of the Square. The streets were almost deserted and only an odd newspaper shop was open. When he reached the Corner Bar he heard animated voices in argument, but before he could cross the street to avoid a meeting, O'Malley the cook stuck his head around the corner and roared.

'O, by the Holy Jesus, here comes the Ballymeara Commie, Cardinal Mindszenty's friend. We were just talking about you. Do you know you were denounced at every Mass in Ballycastle this morning? You were being compared with Judas the Hammer, the man who drove the nails through the blessed palms!'

'It's not a very obvious comparison,' said Martin thinking of how best to steer the conversation away from himself. The Mate and two other men were standing on the sheltered side of the corner reading the *Sunday Empire News*. Murty Griffin had made the front page again! The Mate began to whoop with satisfaction. 'Sweet sanctified Jesus, just wait till Nature hears this one.' He handed Martin the paper.

Under a banner headline that read A REPUBLIC FOR THE HOMELESS AND HELPLESS? and a strapline that said, simply, OLD IRA MAN SLEEPS ON THE WATERS, ran Murty's story:

> Tomorrow in Ballycastle the Republic of Ireland (1949 model) will be proclaimed. Bands will play, speeches will be made, Masses and the Proclamation of 1916 will be read. New memorials will be raised alongside memorials of the War of Independence and the Civil War. And in the Sickeen, where the poor of the town are housed, two families sit in terror, awaiting the bailiff's knock, a knock which will put the parents and their twelve children on the side of the road. BECAUSE THEY OWE THIRTEEN POUNDS RENT.

'The boy is good, so he is,' said the Cook. 'He's fucking-well brilliant.'

> And when the charitable ladies of Ballycastle collect the money, as they have promised, they might spare a thought for a hero of the War of Independence who is spending the end of his days in a filthy hole where the charitable ladies wouldn't put their dogs. Thomas Mac-Dermott, who saw action in seven ambushes, lives in an

old hulk in Ballycastle dock which might sink at any moment. Readers of this newspaper will remember the honours which were bestowed on him some years ago when he tried to rescue a car-load of people who were trapped at the bottom of the dock. When our correspondent in Ballycastle spoke to Mr MacDermott last night he said, 'Another winter would see me in the grave. I'm afraid it's the County Home for me.' And tomorrow they will proclaim the republic in Ballycastle. Do they know the meaning of the word *SHAME*?

'Nature will go stark mad,' said Martin. 'Griffin is a terrible man!'

'An anti-Christ from birth,' said the Mate heartily. His new suit was creased and wrinkled and the seat of his pants covered with red dye from tops of porter barrels on which he had sat.

'I thought you were going south to a wedding?' said Martin.

All the men laughed heartily.

'Divil the wedding,' said the Cook. 'But I'd say he has turned a fair few gallons of porter into water since yesterday morning.'

'The wedding isn't till Tuesday,' said the Mate. 'But whisper me this will you. I missed a fair slice of yesterday but when I came to last night I heard someone say you knocked down the statue of St Anthony in the porch of the Franciscan Church and kicked the head around the road. But of course when I went down this morning to see the damage it was standing there and not even a chip off it.'

'That's Ballycastle for you,' said Martin and made his excuses. He hadn't gone very far when he heard one of the men explaining in a low voice.

'Not at all, I tell you! He fucked the priest first and *then* hit him a belt. That's when he shouted, "And fuck Mindszenty too!" whatever the hell that poor hoor did to him!'

Martin headed quickly for Mrs Anderson's. He wanted

101

to have a good story ready for her so that he could remove his belongings without paying his debts, particularly if she had heard of his outbursts in the church. He felt trapped in a snare which he had helped to set himself and there and then made up his mind to go home with his brother that evening and make some sort of arrangement with his mother about his immediate future. This would give him a steady income, perhaps a car and at least his freedom at weekends. He would clear his debts and make his peace with Nuala. Then he remembered Larry de Lacy! He was chasing around in circles again, in spite of yesterday's resolutions.

He had his hand on Mrs Anderson's door when he noticed that the key was not in the lock, as it usually was by day. He put his hand through the letter-box and began to grope for the brass chain on which the key was fastened. No sooner had his hand appeared than the children gave a warning scream in unison.

'Mammy! Mammy! He's here, he's here!' And they ran from the stairs to the kitchen. They must have been lying in wait for him! He heard Mrs Anderson rushing from the kitchen muttering furiously to herself. She came to the letter-box and began to shriek.

'Have you got my money, you backstreet gutty? If you have you better shove it through the letter-box and clear off from my door. I'll put your old things out later and you can collect them. Do you hear me?'

Not alone could Martin hear her but so also could a group of people who were gathering on the other side of the road, on their way home from Mass, looking in amazement at this strange confrontation through the letter-box. Martin tried to handle the situation as gently as he could.

'Listen to me for a moment, for God's sake, Mrs Anderson. I want to tell you I'm ashamed of what happened in the church last night. I'll go back today and apologise to the priest. And about your money. . . .'

'What in the name of God are you talking about? Have you gone mad entirely? What priest? What church? What

102

nonsense is this?' She was angrier than he ever remembered her and yet she seemed to be totally ignorant of what he was talking about. How strange, he thought, that for once in her life a gobbet of gossip had escaped her. But she was still screaming through the letter-box and the crowd on the other side of the road was getting bigger.

'Go away this minute and don't come back until you have my money in your hand. Get going now or I'll have the police on you.'

She meant it too and Martin didn't wait to ask if Billy was inside, in case affairs which were already serious took yet another turn for the worse. He turned and walked away briskly. But before he had gone very far Mrs Anderson opened the door slightly, stuck her head out and addressed the crowd.

'May the good God look down on the poor widows of the world!'

She banged the door and left the crowd whispering and wondering what it was all about.

Martin headed for Monivea in a state of complete confusion. He would have to get to Nuala before anyone else got to her. A series of extreme solutions to his problems occurred to him. He could ask Nuala to marry him in a year's time, when he would have established peace at home and with a bit of luck and hard work have a degree? He could get his hands on the two properties if he used his head properly and live the life of Riley? The thought had occurred to him before but now necessity gave it a credibility which it previously lacked. But the moment Nuala's mother opened the door he realised that one of his problems, at least, was being taken out of his hands. She was a tall nervous woman in her early forties who was about to lose her good looks but still managed to retain them. As soon as she saw him she put her hands to her throat and screamed.

'You!' she said. 'You! Get away from here this minute! And don't ever come back! Nuala has gone to her Granny's and it's a good job for you that her father is with her this minute. We know everything now. Keep away from our Nuala or you'll be sorry.' She began to heave and gasp with rage and hissed, 'Get off now and go back to your . . . your common prostitutes!'

What was this about? Martin was struck dumb with surprise. Could O'Grady have spread some sort of wild rumour about him? Then the lunatic side of the situation struck him and another wild thought. She was alone in the house. What would happen if he tried to mount her there and then in the hallway? He burst out laughing and Mrs Ryan slammed the heavy door in his face.

For the second time in the space of a half-hour, Martin turned his back on an inhospitable door and headed towards town. What had the woman been talking about? If she had heard of the events in the church what had prostitutes got to do with them? But in spite of the mystery he had to laugh when he thought of the plans he had been considering a few minutes before he arrived at the door. What procrastination had failed to resolve was now resolved in a moment and without any conscious effort of his. Could Billy have been involved in some way? He was inclined to suspect as much and headed for Maggie Fleming's public house.

Maggie didn't believe in after-hours or Sunday opening so Martin went to the kitchen door. When Maggie saw him it was she who wanted information.

'In the name of God, Martin, will you tell me what yourself and Billy are up to at all? His brother, the pilot, came in here last night at about seven o'clock drunk out of his mind and the shop full of customers. He had Billy's baggage and he threw the lot there on the floor. Nothing but effing and blinding and calling Mrs Anderson names that I couldn't repeat if I wanted to. I had to give him a glass of whiskey and then he staggered off and left all the bags here behind him. What's going on at all, Martin?'

Her curiosity was getting the better of her concern. Both of them laughed together and Martin told her of the previous night's adventure with the priest. But these she had heard of from a neighbour on her way home from Mass.

'It's not that at all,' she said. 'That happened about nine, I'm told, but Billy's bags were here two hours before. I'm thinking the brother had to fork out the digs money too as far as I could make out between the curses!'

At that moment a group of men on bicycles came up the street whooping and shouting slogans. Martin remembered the match. Whatever happened he couldn't miss that.

'Look Maggie, I'll ring you this evening. If he turns up in the meantime don't give him his bags until he tells you everything and tell him I want to see him too.'

'Stay on the Cemetery side of the field, Martin,' said Maggie. 'It's hard to say whether your own story or Murty Griffin's story in the paper is the biggest in the town today. You're better off to keep out of sight until people get something else to talk about. God bless you, Martin!'

And Martin joined the big crowd of pedestrians and cyclists heading towards the match and the expected mayhem.

2

The Brothers Pearse, the town team, trotted on to the field together as the referee blew the third blast on his whistle. Their green jerseys were freshly washed and ironed, their togs were spotless and their socks matched. They carried numbers on the backs of their jerseys and new crests bearing the profiles of the Brothers Pearse on their chests. Some people said the crests brought little honour to the dead patriots as these jerseys were often soaked in at least as much blood as was spilt in the Rising of 1916! These cynics were careful not to utter such heresy while Canon Wallace was in earshot. The Canon walked on to the field with his usual pomposity carrying the official list of players. It was written in Irish and the paper was of Irish manufacture. Mattie MacHugh followed a few paces behind him, carrying an armful of hurling sticks and looking around curiously as if he had never before seen the place. The Canon smiled his official smile at the referee, a miserable-looking little fellow, who coveted the little authority which came his way during a downtrodden existence. He cringed and fawned like a pet dog and would have undoubtedly licked the Canon's boots had he been instructed to do so.

'The list, Peter,' said the Canon. 'I hope I find you well, God bless you!'

'I am, thanks be to God, Canon. Your nephew is filling out so he is. I haven't seen him stripped since September.'

The Canon, the referee and Mattie MacHugh looked towards the goal where the Pearses were pucking the ball about. They singled out a young man who had number 14 on his back. He was tall and lanky and his legs were almost as white as his togs. The ball came towards him rapidly on the ground and he returned it neatly between the posts. The three men smiled at each other and shook their heads.

'You'll . . . keep an eye on him. You understand what I mean!' said the Canon quietly but with definite authority. 'It's a sort of friendly encounter in a way but. . . .' The referee's eyes met Mattie MacHugh's for a second and they both looked back at the young man.

'Certainly, Canon. I'll do my almighty best. But, Canon, I've only two eyes. . . .' The Canon put a hand on his shoulder and smiled officially again. 'I am depending on you, Peter!' he said.

The referee coughed meekly as words failed him and the Canon turned and strolled majestically towards the sideline. Mattie MacHugh gave the referee a last pitying glance and followed the Canon. The referee put the whistle in his mouth and began to let off piercing blasts towards the empty goalmouth. He kept this up for some minutes while glancing furiously at his watch. Some of the Pearses' supporters began to shout, 'Walk-over, ref,' and, 'Where's the Kipeen Burke hiding?' The Bawnmore followers answered them in kind. Some of the taunts and slogans were laden with history, both national and local, and the journalists nudged one another. This had to be a clattering match and there would be great lineage from the Dublin dailies.

A gaggle of men could be seen making their way slowly into the ground. They were wearing faded saffron jerseys and togs of varying shades. Twenty years previously the Bawnmore team had to flee the ground during a fight with the Pearses and their supporters, leaving their clothes in the dressing-room. The soldiers from the barracks joined forces with the Pearses that day to rout Bawnmore and a deadly feud was born. Ever since that day, when the Bawnmore teams played in Castletown, they togged out in a house belonging to a couple from the parish, across the road from the ground.

It was all part of parish history and it kept the old feud alive. Apart from keeping the feud alive and ensuring that the team took the field in a suitably bloodthirsty mood, the custom was now unnecessary. The team walked slowly and menacingly towards the referee who was still whistling angrily and pointing a finger at his watch. His actions didn't seem to interest them at all and it was very obvious from their appearance that the occasion didn't inspire their respect either. Their jerseys looked as if they had been stowed in a sack since their last muddy outing and their togs were daubed with grass-stains and dollops of cow-dung. Most of them wore peak caps and as they walked they pulled viciously with their sticks at lumps of mud and stray thistles. They carried no numbers on their backs and their hurley sticks were bound with tin bands and coils of thatching rope. They kept advancing on the little referee glaring venomously but not quickening their pace at all, in spite of his furious whistling.

The Pearses stood in a huddle behind the referee watching their old enemies coming towards them. Most eyes were fastened on the one man. The Kipeen Burke stood about five foot seven but he was so broad of shoulder, and so beefy from hip to ankle, that he looked even smaller when he stood on his own. His body was covered with thick black hair and even when clean-shaven his jowls glistened darkly. When playing he wore a peak cap turned back to front, his knees were bound in bandages and he wore a broad leather strap on his left wrist. But the Kipeen's mouth was the most terrifying part of his extraordinary body. As a result of countless blows he had lost all his teeth and his lips and gums were scarred. When he wore his dentures the damage was not so noticeable and he looked quite human: but when he removed them his appearance changed utterly and when he bared his hacked gums to charge a player or to meet a ball as it fell from the air, he was truly frightening to behold. To add to the effect his speech seemed hardly human without the teeth, particularly when he flew into a rage, something which happened frequently. Eighteen years previously, when he had got a regular place on the county senior team, he called the Canon, 'the leavings of a bailiff's prick' during an argument after an unfinished match against the Army.

Some people believed the Canon was the illegitimate son of the local Lord's steward but it was something they kept far from their lips whatever about their thoughts. But the Kipeen shouted it loud and clear where hundreds heard him and his fate as a county hurler was sealed. From that day on he was rarely picked for the county and the Canon did his best to get him out of hurling altogether. Once he succeeded in getting Bawnmore banned for six months because of some technicality but they bided their time and returned. The Kipeen was always a rough player but now, at the age of forty-three with his mind full of accumulated spites and venom, he was more lethal than a platoon of soldiers. When he first heard the Canon's nephew was picked for the match he thought his leg was being pulled. When he discovered it was true he came to the conclusion that the Canon had taken leave of his senses.

The two teams gathered around the referee and the catcalling started. The Kipeen called for silence and addressed him formally.

'Will spindle-shanks here take his bottle at half-time or will it do in the hospital after the match?' Patrick Pearse

MacCarthy flushed with shame and anger and attempted to glare at the Kipeen but what he saw in his face sent a shudder of fear through him.

The referee blew a very long blast on his whistle to get silence.

'The first man to strike an opponent with his hurley goes to the line without warning. Do you understand that clearly, Kipeen Burke?'

'I was baptised too, shitty bollocks,' said the Kipeen, with terrifying friendliness. Then someone farted loudly.

'A salute to the Republic,' shouted the Kipeen. 'Every man take a man and if you put a foot inside the twenty-one-yard line you'll be taken out of this ground feet first,' and he pointed his hurley at Patrick Pearse MacCarthy.

The referee had whipped out his notebook to take the Kipeen's name when he realised he hadn't started the game. This increased his anger and doing his best to gain control of the situation he roared, 'Backs back! Backs back!' Seven men from each side ran towards the two goals to defend but a murmur ran through the crowd when the Kipeen didn't move at all. He remained standing in the middle of the field, leaning on his stick and staring at the referee. Spectators and players alike stood in total silence and it was the Kipeen himself who broke it.

'Nobody told us anything about a minute's silence for those who died for this Republic of yours. Start the game you fucking eejit and don't stand there like an imbecile.'

The referee felt a leaden load descend on his shoulders and the pit of his stomach seemed to fill with cold water. He looked foolishly around him.

'Why aren't you playing where you always play? Aren't you playing full-back?'

'I'm playing full-forward, you wet dream,' said the Kipeen. 'I'm very sorry but the number must have come off my jersey in the laundry!'

The Bawnmore players began to stagger about with exaggerated roars of laughter which quickly changed to wild whoops which their supporters took up on the sidelines. The referee looked imploringly at the Canon who was staring with open mouth from the sideline. Then he blew his whistle, shut his eyes and threw in the ball.

To this day nobody can say with complete certainty what happened next, not even some of the players involved. The referee didn't open his eyes again until the following day for he was engulfed by the mêlée, knocked to the ground and, whether by accident or design, kicked in the back of the head. The players from both sides got to grips with opponents and began to hit and kick and yell at the tops of their voices. The backs and a crowd from the sidelines all rushed to the middle of the field but the Canon was too late to save his nephew. Two of the Bawnmore players took hold of him and the Kipeen buried the handle of his stick under his floating ribs and stretched him cold.

But while all this was happening on the field, the section of the crowd who came to watch the action raised another cry. It was then noticed that a party of Bawnmore supporters had snatched the Republican Cup from a table on the sidelines and were running away with it out of the ground. Then someone shouted an order to the Bawnmore players and they too began to fight a rearguard action out of the ground. The Canon stood stock still, one eye on his vanishing trophy and the other on his unconscious nephew. A lorry pulled up outside the gate and the Bawnmore team and some of their supporters climbed on. In a matter of seconds the Republican Cup was heading towards Bawnmore and the dishonourable ceremonies which were going to greet its arrival.

3

Father Brendan Melody was sitting impatiently and uncomfortably in the large hall that passed for a lounge in the Royal Hotel on the Square. He deeply regretted having agreed to meet his brother in this place for a meeting which

110

was going to be very unpleasant. It was much more like the waiting-room of a large railway station than a hotel lounge. The bus depot was just around the corner and the hotel was useful as a meeting-place for travellers with the result that it was almost always crowded. There was a bar at one end of the lounge but it was closed on Sunday. Father Brendan tried to get into a smaller lounge upstairs but found it had been commandeered by the Fianna Fáil councillors and their hangers-on. Under the chairmanship of Deputy Peterson they were planning their course of action for the following day. Large trays full of illegally procured whiskey were being ferried in to them as they discussed the procedures to be followed at the High Mass and whether they should march to and from the church individually or as a body. Father Brendan sought refuge in the most discreet corner of the huge lounge which was now rapidly filling with people just back from the abandoned match. He was careful not to get involved in the lively discussions but gathered that the Canon was disgraced and the trophy stolen. Good! Perhaps the bishop would at last do something about this nonsense. There was still no sign of his brother and he made up his mind to get him across the Square to the Railway Hotel, where he could tear strips off him in some sort of privacy.

But when Martin breezed in he was still laughing heartily and all things, good and bad, forgotten for the moment except the hilarious sights he had just seen. He sat down and began to give his brother all the news.

'Sorry I'm late but Murty Griffin, the reporter, gave me a lift to Bawnmore on the back of his motorbike to see the action. The kids are belting the Canon's cup around the village with hurleys. They're preparing a concrete bed for whatever is left of it in the wall at the back of the parish hall. It's where the men come out to piss during dances! They're a wild crowd I tell you! You heard the news about Dad of course?'

Only then did Martin realise his brother was seething with anger. He couldn't understand why, particularly since

111

he had visited his father just before the operation. Father Brendan took a very deep breath and squeezed his jaws so hard that a red roll of flesh rose up over his collar. He began to speak in a heavy, measured way like a bad actor indicating that he was about to lose his temper.

'Would you mind leaving this terrible place and coming with me to the Railway Hotel? There are things to be discussed . . . very, very important things, believe me. This place is much too public!'

I have you, you bloody reptile, said Martin to himself and this time I'll squeeze. So he said, as casually as he could, 'I see nothing wrong with this place. Anything I have to say can be said here!'

His false casualness increased his brother's rage considerably. He took a grip of his kneecaps, shoved his head across the little table that was between them and began to hiss at Martin.

'Listen to me, now! I know everything. Everything! I visited Mrs Anderson and called on the Bursar and spent a most embarrassing half-hour with Father Alphonsus in the Friary. That's how I spent the day, you blackguard while you . . . you . . . shhhh. . . .' His voice rose and he began to wave his hands. Then, in an effort to control his temper he exhaled suddenly and made a sound like air escaping from a badly-punctured tyre. Two women who were drinking tea noisily at a table nearby stopped suddenly, cups in mid-air. I have you, thought Martin and I'll squeeze you until your ribs crack. But his brother hadn't played his trump card.

He put his hand in his waistcoat pocket, concealed something in his fist, which he then held clenched in front of Martin. Then with a quick glance around the room, he opened his fist for a split second, closed it again and put the object back in his waistcoat pocket. Martin rose to his feet with shock and stared at his brother's waistcoat. So many things became clear to him at once, that he thought his head would burst. For what his brother had so fleetingly shown him was one of the French letters Billy

O'Grady had thrown across the room to him on Good Friday morning.

'Oh, holy fuck!' he said, loudly and involuntarily. The two women again stopped drinking tea and began to stare at him.

'Sit down, you galoot!' Father Brendan was turning scarlet with rage and shame. 'Let's get out of here fast!' Martin sat down just as his brother rose and he had to sit down again suddenly. Martin found some relief in a burst of nervous laughter.

'We're rehearsing a play,' he said to the women. 'Be sure and come to the Town Hall to see it!'

They put down their cups, gathered their belongings and fled but the diversion gave Martin a chance to recover from this last hammer-blow. Already his brother had launched into another attack. These were the final proposals!

'Your bags are in my car. Mrs Anderson has been paid. Your pub debts and whatever other money you owe are matters for yourself. Shut your mouth, I say, and keep it shut until I finish! I apologised to the Franciscans and you will write them a letter which I'll dictate. We go straight home now and never, never, as long as she lives will Mammy hear a word about all this. You'll start work in the shop tomorrow and we'll make a proper financial settlement with you . . . on a week-to-week basis. Shut up, I tell you! There are a few things to be said. You'll stay away from Billy O'Grady and you'll also keep clear of this foul town. If you want to see Nuala Ryan . . . if she is fool enough to want to see you ever again . . . you can invite her home. But all this is urgent now. Mammy and I are taking Dad to Lourdes as soon as the wound has healed.'

Martin looked so shocked that the priest halted his outburst.

'You can't be serious?' Father Brendan brushed him aside.

'Look! That's no concern of yours at all. One way or another we meant to take him there, I'm only telling you now so that you'll realise the importance of . . . of getting all these sordid little details out of the way once and for all.'

But Martin had ceased to think of himself and was now thinking of his father as he saw him the previous day. The fine head on the rapidly decaying body, the pain he was trying to conceal and the terrible final struggle with death that lay ahead. The blood seemed to leave his head and for the first time in his life he felt undiluted anger.

'You bastard! You fucking bastard!'

The venom in the voice and the mad glare in the soft blue eyes frightened the priest. The fact that he knew Martin to be cold sober increased his fear. But a surge of anger soon obliterated it.

'Don't push your luck, you little pup! Use that word again and I'll pull the windpipe out of you. You're not in the company of tramps and their sluts now. You're speaking to one of God's anointed and don't forget it again!'

All eyes and ears were on them now but the brothers had forgotten the audience. Those of them who knew Martin were nudging and whispering of his other escapades in the town. It was a great day for gossip!

'Listen to me, then! Why can't you let my father die in some sort of comfort? Why can't you stop that heartless bitch from taking him out there to salve her own conscience? Did either of you ask him about it at all? Well, I'm telling you this, you'll not be let away with this one!'

'You're very concerned about him now, thanks be to God,' said the priest with savage sarcasm. 'You who didn't bother to visit him for two whole months until yesterday.'

'And do you want to know why? Do you? Whether you do or not I'm going to tell you. I was afraid if I met yourself or my mother in there that I'd lose my temper and say things I should have said long ago . . . the things I'm saying to you now, you tub of guts! And if you ever again threaten to hit me I'll kick the shite out through your ribs.'

The priest recoiled. He drew his head down between his shoulders and looked apprehensively around the lounge like a badger trapped in his den. Those who were sitting

114

around the lounge were hiding behind newspapers or studying the ceiling or floor intently with ears cocked to the limit. Father Brendan made a final bid for peace.

'Please don't disgrace us completely. Think of your father on his death-bed. Come to a quiet place with me! Don't refuse me!'

But Martin had stopped listening to him although he seemed to be staring into his eyes.

'Answer me one question, just one question. When my mother put Mary into the Home why didn't you stop her? Where was your Christianity then? Or did you advise her and help her because you figured it wouldn't help your chances of an early parish if it was known that your sister was up the pole. . . ?

'I know now who has you primed. It's that anti-Christ Larry de Lacy. That filthy old degenerate . . . living with a coloured woman in New York. Oh, you can collect them all right! They gather on you like maggots on a corpse.'

Martin reacted with a taunting grin and began to bait his brother as if he were teasing a dog.

'So that's what it is after all! I never really believed it but the old cock really troubles you. So you envy Larry the black woman. Well, I suppose she'd be an improvement on your old housekeeper. She must be overdue for a rebore. And I didn't believe Larry when he said you were stripping the nurses in the hospital with your eyes.'

The priest bounded out of his chair and Martin thought he was going to catch him by the throat. As his brother was much heavier than he was he decided to dive out of his chair on to the floor. But as he was about to dive his brother rushed out the door and across the Square. Martin ran after him for he had a few books in his baggage that he didn't wish to lose. But when he reached the car he found his brother throwing his bags on to the pavement. He threw his overcoat on top of them and banged the lid of the boot. Then he turned and spat into his brother's face.

'May you never have a day's luck,' he said. 'Never! Never! Never!'

115

Martin made no attempt to remove the spit and he spoke quietly although his voice was quavering with emotion.

'This is for the last Sunday in July, in 1938,' he said and hit his brother as hard as he could into the pit of the stomach. Then he gathered his bags and coat and walked across the Square leaving his brother groaning on the pavement.

But when he reached the Four Masters Hotel his rage had drained and he felt weak and inclined to tremble. The sound of drunken voices came from the back bar, although the front bar seemed locked. He thought a drink might do him good and then he decided not to have one. He was about to change his mind again when Stella Walsh came towards him from the dining-room. She was dressed in her Sunday best and looked very cheerful. She noticed Martin's distress although he tried to pass it off as a thing of no consequence.

'The brother and myself had it out at last. I lost my temper and hit him. I won't bore you with the details.'

She looked sad and displeased. Physical violence frightened her and she took to her heels at the first sign of a fight. But very few fights took place in the hotel, mainly because most of the customers were more interested in other forms of physical contact.

'I think I'll have a drink to settle myself.'

'Not just now. Leave your bags upstairs and when you come down I'll feed you in the dining-room. And afterwards if you take me for a walk to the Golden Strand, I'll let you have two drinks. Isn't that fair?'

He said it was very fair and took his bags to his room. Already the memory of the blow he gave his brother was beginning to dim and he understood that it really signified the end of something. When he came down the stairs again he felt calmer than he had felt for a long time.

MONDAY

18

APRIL
1949

1

Martin couldn't recollect a more pleasant awakening. He was lying naked on his back with the sun streaming through the curtains. Stella lay face down beside him with her head in the crook of his left arm. She was also naked and fast asleep. Pleasure at last, he thought and not before its time either. He eased gently down under the sheet, stretched and eased his arm down under her neck. She grunted and turned her head towards him so that he could feel her even breath on his skin. He was somewhat surprised at the ease with which he accepted these new circumstances. His conscience didn't trouble him at all although his mind, conditioned by family upbringing and education, told him he should feel remorseful and guilty. Everything happened in such an unhurried and unplanned way that he remembered no conscious decision by either of them to go to bed together. That was just another phase of their evening together: the walk to Golden Strand and back, the drinks and the talk that went on and on until early morning. There was but the slightest hesitation at the door of his room and suddenly, and without a word being spoken, the bed was filled with limbs that twined and untwined, lips and tongues that met and roamed and met again and loins that pressed and thrust until a wild and sudden coupling brought release and a great calm.

A warm excitement filled his groin again as he recalled the pleasure that became more intense and more prolonged after his first clumsy possession of her body. Stella realised that she had brought him his first fulfilment and it increased her pleasure greatly.

'I took you first,' she said. 'I had you before that rich bitch on the hill!'

But he no longer felt loyalty to Nuala or the least regret for what was happening. Indeed, he was beginning to take pleasure out of the envy of two women who had never met. He was able to compare their bodies in a dispassionate way. Stella was small compared with Nuala and could not be described as beautiful. Her face, her breasts, her limbs and particularly her hard and muscular buttocks were all small and spherical. As his hands caressed her during the night he told her of his first memory of her; a story which could have seemed coarse in different circumstances. He was standing outside the Corner Bar when a girl passed by wearing a very tight pair of slacks. A voice laden with lust groaned, 'Sweet suffering Jesus, look! Wouldn't you know by the cut of that one's arse that she carries a powerful engine!' Stella laughed again and again and after a silence that was filled with sensuality, touched him urgently and said, 'Start it again, Martin and let's go for a spin!'

And she told him it was his mouth that attracted her the first night he came to the hotel with Billy and his brother. She was trying to imagine how his mouth would feel on hers when she felt Billy's eyes roaming over her and when their eyes met he leered knowingly and she knew he had read her thoughts. For a long time after that he pursued her.

'I've nothing against him, in fact I've hardly any feelings at all about him. Some men talk who have something to tell . . . and that's bad enough . . . but Billy tells stories about girls who never walked a yard of road with him.' But she did understand how Billy got his women. 'The ugliest man in Ireland would get women if he was as easily pleased as Billy . . . and as difficult to insult.'

118

She also told him about Wally Watson, an English musician who came to Ireland to dodge the Army and the war and who was her first lover. She always sought and enjoyed male company, particularly as her aunt was intensely puritanical. But her own physical responses to their advances frightened her. She was terrified that a moment's total surrender to the warmth and love she sought could end in the laundry of the Magdalene Home, where the unmarried mothers of the town were rehabilitated and steamed for twelve months. The lonely little Englishman showed her how this fate could be avoided. They both sought tenderness and found it together. But when she was being bridesmaid at her sister's wedding she confessed her sin and was refused absolution when she wouldn't promise not to see Watson again.

Some time later his old girlfriend came over from England and they got married. Although he had since sought to renew their relationship she refused, but remained on friendly terms with him. She also resumed the practice of her religion but in a half-hearted and very personal way and she also kept her men at a distance and discouraged permanent relationships.

Martin was pleased when she encouraged him to tell her about his own problems. She was particularly interested in his sister and asked him if he wasn't anxious to see her now that he knew where she was. He said there was nothing he wanted more and then she said that it might be good for him to go immediately and ask her for advice. She would certainly want to attend her father's funeral (an occasion which might well come sooner than anyone expected) and would find it much easier to return with one of the family than on her own. It all sounded so simple and so logical that he wondered why he hadn't already decided on it himself. Perhaps his father was also thinking of this when he gave Larry that sum of money. . . . Dawn was already brightening the chinks in the curtains when they both slid into a deep sleep.

He stole a glance at his watch without moving his arm too

much but the slight movement was sufficient to waken her.

'It's ten o'clock,' he whispered. 'Do you have to get up immediately?' She shook her head drowsily and tried to rub the sleep out of her eyes against the point of his shoulder. Then she pressed her mouth against his ear and whispered, 'Martin, do you have any of those left?' And later, when she began to move against him as she approached her climax the intensity and violence of her desire for his body took him by surprise and frightened him a little. But that passed quickly and he abandoned himself completely to the new and exhausting pleasure. And when he lay spent beside her, about to sink into sleep again, he thought he felt tears that were not his own drying on his cheek. But when he tried to speak to her she told him sharply not to be so silly and so vain and go to sleep. And when he woke again he was alone in the bed.

His breakfast was waiting when he came downstairs. They had the place to themselves for the hotel was never noted for early rising, even on week-days. Again he began to search for feelings of contrition or shame but all he really felt was a deep affection for this neat little girl who was looking after him so well.

'It's a quarter to twelve. The High Mass will start at noon, across the road and the action on the Square afterwards. You may as well go seeing as you're so near at hand. I'd go with you myself but the manageress left a note saying that she wouldn't be back until late evening. I'll have to mind the castle in case the valuables are stolen . . . and if you say that I'm the most valuable thing in the house I'll kick you in the teeth!'

As he finished eating the bell for Mass began to toll and he got up to go. When Stella stretched to unbolt the front door he put his arms around her but she shook her head.

'Not now, Martin, please don't. I think you know why. I'll see you this evening.' She gave his hand a squeeze as he passed her and fastened the door again. He walked up the alleyway to the Pro-Cathedral and the Catholic Church's official blessing on the new Republic.

Bishop Mullin was in a very bad mood. He sat uneasily on his scarlet throne scowling sideways at the congregation with unconcealed disfavour. His flock were able to ascertain, with a fair degree of accuracy, what frame of mind their Bishop was in by looking at the gap between his nose and his chin. These two outstanding features of his countenance were threatening to meet since birth, but age and good living had increased their size and made them even more conspicuous. When nose and chin looked like making instant contact it was high time for the Bishop's enemies to take to the trenches. His enemies were varied and numerous: writers of bad books (particularly Irish writers) and those who read them, English Sunday newspapers, men and women who swam from the same beaches, anyone who could see the slightest virtue in any tenet of Socialism, women who wore slacks or shorts, Irish Protestants who demanded their constitutional rights aggressively, and public representatives or officials who didn't obey his instructions immediately, for Bishop Mullin never gave advice. When they didn't expose their bodies excessively in public or accentuate their more sinful protuberances, Bishop Mullin paid little attention to women. Indeed, he doubted that any woman who wasn't a legitimate mother could claim full equality with man in the eyes of God. He was totally opposed to giving them any authority outside of the family.

But the Bishop's prejudices were not confined to the laity. He bore a particular grudge against any priest who considered himself an intellectual, particularly if he belonged to an order and seemed to side-step the Bishop's authority. Young priests in his diocese who read a lot or who wrote articles for intellectual journals were soon steered into other activities such as staging religious plays, organising football teams, running the St Vincent de Paul Society or drinking discreetly after hours in places where important information might be let slip. The religious orders were careful not to transfer any of their more controversial members to Ballycastle. Instead they sent pious old men in their dotage or silly young ones who started movements to canonise obscure Spanish flagellants or write pamphlets for the Catholic Truth Society about the devil in dance halls or the use of the cold, wet towel as a cure for involuntary pollution. With the appointment of Monsignor Blake as President, Bishop Mullin had reduced the University to a satisfactory state of mediocrity. And through a network of religious espionage, based on the confraternities, half the population was spying on the other half.

But all this didn't mean that Bishop Mullin had eliminated all problems in his diocese At this very moment he was waiting impatiently for High Mass to reach the point when he would address the congregation. The recent change of Government upset him and the new Republic annoyed him. He distrusted new things simply because they upset tried and trusted patterns of thought and action. He had already found that this present Government was as susceptible to episcopal pressures as the de Valera Government and perhaps even more so. But this new Republic nearly started a religious conflict in the town. The gap between nose and chin narrowed again. He looked down at the seat where the Fianna Fáil contingent sat, shepherded by Deputy Peterson. That fellow had the cheek to tell him that his party was thinking of boycotting the High Mass! He soon put an end to that piece of nonsense but it showed how careful one had to be.

His sharp eyes darted over the congregation and lit on another enemy, Murty Griffin, who was sitting in one of the front seats with his head and arms thrown forward on the rail in front of him. Fast asleep, no doubt! A young woman with a blouse so low-cut that the Bishop could see half-way down the cleft between her breasts knelt beside him.

It was three years now since Murty Griffin got under Bishop Mullin's feet for the first time. He had issued a Lenten Pastoral in which he stated that anyone who attended a dance that went on after midnight in his diocese, during Lent, committed a mortal sin. Some time later he was shown a story in an English Sunday newspaper which told of lorry-loads of people leaving the diocese of Bally-castle to dance without fear of damnation across the diocesan boundary. When he found that Murty Griffin was the source, and when he had decided on a way to muzzle him permanently, a serious matter was brought to his notice. Murty had a crazy aunt who lived alone in a huge house outside the town and who was promising her parish priest three stained glass windows for the new Cathedral, as soon as the foundation stone was laid. That changed everything, for the time being, but as soon as the bequest was delivered Murty would be dealt with. All this reminded Bishop Mullin of an incident from the previous day and he wrote a note in the margin of his sermon.

When the Bishop went towards the pulpit everyone, inside and outside the church, snapped out of the stupor they were in since Mass began. Those who were standing outside in the sunshine with their backs to the wall rushed into the porch to listen. This was undoubtedly the most interesting part of the ceremony. Martin slipped through the crowd and made his way to a statue under which he found Nature sitting alone. Because of the overpowering stench of his body and clothes there was always plenty of room near him in church.

Murty Griffin roused himself, took out his notebook and put it on his knee. Nancy looked at him proudly. It was her first time with him on official business and it was almost like being married. Indeed some of the thoughts she entertained as she day-dreamed through Mass had nothing at all to do with matters of the spirit.

The Bishop stood silently for a time staring contemptuously at the congregation. Most of them would not be too surprised if he told them some Sunday that he didn't give a fig for themselves or their souls. When the last nervous cough had died down and the last fidgeting foot stilled, he started off in his usual low key.

It had been an outstanding year in the town's history; two weeks ago the Holy Father had sent a special blessing to Ballycastle because of the outstanding part the faithful had played in the cause of Cardinal Mindszenty who was suffering so much for the Faith. Martin crouched into his nook under the statue and kept his eyes on the floor. The town councillors swelled with pride. The resolution they had passed about the imprisonment of the Cardinal exceeded all others in the Catholic world in malevolence of sentiment and virulence of language. First trick to the Bishop, thought the Faithful! He then gave a cursory lambasting to all forms of Socialism, Communism and State Control of education.

Then, raising his voice slightly, he praised those who were engaged in collecting money for some needy families in the town. This was good and Christian work. They were very praiseworthy endeavours. However, it was necessary to enunciate certain principles clearly, in case well-intentioned and charitable people were unaware of them. All ears homed in on the Bishop's words and Murty Griffin's pencil was at the ready. Here came the first salvo.

'I would like to remind you, dear people, that Catholic charity should carry the stamp of the Catholic community and that our St Vincent de Paul Society is the recognised and proper channel for such charity, in this town as it is in other towns. This is not to say, of course, that other religious denominations cannot have charitable organisations of their own. In fact, my dear people, many of them are rightly noted for the diligence of their charitable societies.'

He paused and all eyes turned towards the Town Clerk's wife who had turned crimson and looked like bursting into tears. Most of the congregation sniggered. Good enough for the meddling bitch and her friend, the Minister's wife! The Bishop cleared his throat and gave a short history of the Catholic Church in Ireland since the time of the Penal Laws. He used big words, obscure technical terms and Latin quotations which he didn't bother translating. He

124

came from Rome to Ballycastle to take over the diocese and local folklore had it that the Pope himself was stunned by his erudition. Indeed, it was said that no more than a handful of Church elders could fully comprehend his thesis on the Assumption of the Blessed Virgin with which he got his doctorate. But now the congregation was getting restless again, anxious for the next personal attack. The Bishop changed course skilfully.

'A sad sign of these modern times, my dear people, is the tendency to denigrate and decry institutions which were dearly won: sometimes, indeed, by the supreme sacrifice. This is part of an international conspiracy whose main purpose is to make ready the path for the advent of atheistic Communism and its attendant reign of terror and bloodshed. Yesterday, in one of these filthy English Sunday newspapers . . . against which I have so often warned you . . . there was a very good example of what I mean. It was a cheap and sneering piece of gutter-journalism which held up to public ridicule the glorious Easter Rising of 1916. But, my dear people, the remedy is in your hands. Don't buy these base and filthy periodicals and make sure not to buy your own newspapers in the shops that offer them for sale.'

Nancy glanced anxiously at Murty but he was clearly furious that the Bishop hadn't named either himself or his paper thus rendering his attack un-newsworthy. Murty knew very well that no newsagent in Ballycastle would stop selling these Sunday papers until every other newsagent had already done so. But he stopped this train of thought for the Bishop was about to sail into the shallow waters of party politics.

'This is a very special day, dear people. Today we can reflect with understandable pride on how this land of ours has progressed since those distant days when the holy sacrifice of the Mass had to be celebrated in secret in remote valleys. All our political parties can be proud of the part they played in our recent history and in their efforts to eliminate injustice and violence from our society.'

125

The councillors were so pleased with this that some of them became suspicious that they were once again to be outflanked and outwitted by the Bishop who seemed to be heading away rapidly from the prickly problems of the new Republic. Their suspicions were well-founded. The Bishop took up his script, glared at it, and tore away at full speed.

'We have just emerged from a bloody World War. A war that devastated whole countries, destroyed their people, smashed their boundaries and in many cases their religious beliefs and culture as well. Millions died; men, women and children. And, my dear people, this country of ours was spared!' Some old women at the bottom of the church were heard to sigh and lament. They were women from Irishtown whose close relatives had perished in various branches of the British armed forces. The Bishop glared in their direction and his nose took another leap towards his chin.

'Let us thank God that we were spared, my dear people. Let us praise the wisdom of those who guided our destinies during those crucial years.' Deputy Peterson smiled broadly and Councillor Macken frowned. 'But let us also praise those political leaders who put the national interest ahead of narrow party interest. That, my dear people, is true patriotism.' Another trick to the Bishop! But some of the congregation were puzzled.

'What tack is he on now?' whispered the Mate to his neighbour in the porch. 'He's skimmed the Republic without knocking a barnacle off it. He's in open sea now! White and clear, boy!' The crowd in the porch strained its ears and craned its necks. Any minute now they would know if it was worth their while hanging around any longer.

'But my dear people, certain questions must now be asked. God in his goodness has granted us a peaceful country where our ancient faith is held in high public esteem. Why then, my dear brethren, do so many of our young people have so little regard for their country that

126

they turn their backs on it, and, for purely materialistic reasons, go to live and work in alien environments where their faith and their morals are in jeopardy? But, my dear people, some of these people go even further and enlist in the armed forces of that country and fight that country's enemies as if they were our enemies. Worse still, this country of their adoption does not hesitate to enter into unholy alliance with the mortal enemies of the faith in defence of which their own forefathers laid down their lives. Think well on it today, beloved people, and offer up your prayers that these unfortunate citizens of this island may see the error of their ways and return to the path of virtue. Let us also pray that peace may flourish in our midst as a result of today's event and that it may not be the unwitting cause of renewing old spleens and feuds. And finally, my dear people, continue to pray daily for that prince of our church who has been incarcerated by the earthly forces of darkness. Your prayers and messages of support have already given him hope in his hour of need. God bless you all.'

The sermon was a great disappointment to everyone. Apart from two personal attacks and another so obscure that nobody got its point fully, it was well below his usual standard. Murty Griffin put away his notebook. The crack about the St Vincent de Paul Society was of no use to him either so he nudged Nancy and beckoned her to a side-door. He had heard Nature was on the warpath and wanted to avoid a public confrontation. Martin and Nature sat under the statue, waiting for the congregation to disperse, while Nature gave him graphic descriptions of the physical changes he hoped to make in Murty's anatomy as soon as he laid hands on him. And when the congregation made their way into the narrow streets around the Pro-Cathedral they didn't dally as they usually did. Most of them headed towards the Square where the new Republic would shortly be proclaimed.

3

The march to the Square was assembling on the bridge at Irishtown. The preparations were watched by a small crowd returning home from Mass who were being greatly entertained by the proceedings. Ballycastle had two marching bands, the St Francis Xavier Brass Band, from the Franciscan Sodality, and the Dockers Fife and Drum Band from Irishtown. The Brass Band was of very recent origin and had so far learned to play three tunes: *The Wearing of the Green, The Three Flowers* and the theme music from the film *Message of Fatima*. However, their uniforms and instruments were brand new and for this reason Councillor Macken put them at the head of the parade, behind the army colour party. The Dockers Band brought up the rear, for all that remained of their original uniforms were their greasy and tattered peak caps. They were good musicians, although most of them boozed heavily and couldn't march in a straight line if the re-unification of Ireland depended on it. They now stood in three ragged lines, seething with anger because of this latest insult. Councillor Macken made an effort to placate them and offered an extra two pounds fee if they stopped complaining. This made them even angrier and their leader, Williameen MacDonough, offered to shove his fife up the Councillor's arse and play *The Geese in the Bog* through his ear-holes, as well as a lot of much coarser offers that caused some mothers to collect their children and head for home. Councillor Macken was scandalised, as well as being furious, and trotted back to the head of the parade muttering about filthy British Army language and how very right the Bishop had been in his sermon.

The town councillors stood foolishly behind the Brass Band. Their robes of office looked even shabbier in daylight than they did in the dimness of the council chamber. Behind them came the other official bodies, from the University, the Red Cross Society, the Knights of Malta, the Catholic Boy Scouts and a small group of Old IRA men who took the Free State side in the Civil War. Just as Councillor Macken was about to give the order to strike up the music, two of the Old IRA men approached him and complained about the lowly place allotted them in the parade, behind a crowd of schoolboys in short pants. The truth of the matter was that Councillor Macken didn't want to draw too much attention to the six old dotards who insisted on marching despite all his pleas. He ran back to them, spitting with rage, but no sooner had he reached their position than the Dockers Band struck up *Roll Out the Barrel* and drowned out everything else completely. Everyone took this to be a signal to march and the parade moved off. Councillor Macken had to gather his robes around his waist and sprint towards the Brass Band shouting at them to play for all they were worth.

As was always the case in Ballycastle the crowd that waited at the Square was composed of three main groups: those who came because of genuine interest, those who came out of curiosity and those who came in the hope of seeing or hearing something outrageous. The first group was the smallest and the third by far the largest. A wooden platform had been specially constructed in the centre of the Square alongside the Memorial which was covered by a white sheet. Loudspeakers were erected in the four corners of the Square and a young man in a broadcasting van near the platform was testing his equipment, 'One, Two, Three'; 'One, Two, Three', while a cluster of little boys chanted 'Go and have a pee' back at him. When they learned that no shots would be fired they lost interest and went off to play a noisy game of football on the green behind the platform.

The small group who came out of genuine interest stood around the platform. The curious ones gathered in the centre of the Square and the others stood scattered along the footpaths or leaning against the railings in front of the bank that faced the platform. And half-way between this group and the platform Sergeant Lynch sat on his bicycle with one leg on the ground, gazing about aimlessly with an idiotic expression on his great moon face.

A stranger to Ballycastle wouldn't waste a second glance on Sergeant Lynch. He was a huge, fleshy, red-haired man and one of the very few recruits with little or no formal education to leave the Training Depot as a Sergeant. According to local folklore he was roused in the dead of night and asked to go to a remote hamlet in County Kerry which had already accounted for three sergeants in less than a year. Lynch took the opportunity and the risk and did so well that after five years the Superintendent offered him his own choice of posting. He asked to be assigned permanently to Ballycastle but refused all offers of promotion. He had spent more than twenty years in the town and if it was true to say that a fly couldn't stir unknown to Bishop Mullin, it was equally true to say, as the Tailor had said, of Sergeant Lynch: 'There isn't a cock that raises its head under a blanket in this town whose movements aren't known to that hoor before it stops spitting.'

He was known locally as 'Bacon' because he had made the villages and townlands east of Ballycastle his own personal precinct. He checked dog and bull licences and arbitrated in the various disputes concerning rights of way and trespass that frequently threatened the peace. The farmers in this area killed their own pigs and cured their bacon. Flitches of bacon hung from the ceilings of the kitchens and Sergeant Lynch lavished his praises on their self-sufficiency and good husbandry. He returned from his expeditions to the country with a bag packed with pieces of bacon, potatoes, vegetables and other assorted loot on the carrier of the bicycle on which he seemed to sit at all times. He suited the country people and they suited him.

Not long after his arrival in Ballycastle a prominent public representative rang the barracks one night with news that not only was illegal drinking on a large scale going on in the Royal Hotel but that an illegal organisation was in session there as well. Sergeant Lynch knew very well that what was going on was a meeting of a local branch of the newly-formed Fianna Fáil party but he summoned two companions and did his duty. He didn't intend doing more than that for he knew that one day Fianna Fáil might well be in power and issuing the same veiled threats. He rang the hotel bell, having heard the sounds of revelry through the letter-box. There was a sudden silence and then a short pause, not long enough to cause him to ring again. Then the door was opened wide by a blonde girl who apologised most charmingly for the delay and invited them in. The bar was closed and locked and the lounge empty except for a group of resident commercial travellers who were playing cards in a corner and drinking lawfully. She invited the policemen to search the other lounges and sitting-rooms if they wished. They accepted the offer but found nothing and nobody. Sergeant Lynch didn't sleep a wink when he came off duty that morning. The cunning and dexterity of this charming girl delighted him and from then on he haunted the bar of the Royal Hotel during his days and nights off. They were married within a year and it was said in Ballycastle that they would live where a periwinkle would perish.

A knot of people gathered around Nature, at the railings of the bank, giving their own interpretations of Murty Griffin's article and advising him about his future dwelling-places. The Tailor was there, Michael Thornton (who hadn't opened the bar so that he wouldn't miss any possible fun, although he told certain customers he was keeping it shut out of respect for the new Republic), Cook O'Malley, Munchie Roche, a crowd in from the country on bicycles and the Mate, looking even more bedraggled than he was the previous day. A short distance away the big German was lying against the railings dressed in the same clothes he was wearing for weeks now. He was absolutely filthy, hadn't shaved for many days and his eyes were bloodshot and rheumy. The Tailor drew attention to him.

'Isn't he a credit to us, lads!' he said to the others. 'When that man came to this town about a year and a half ago he was up before cock-crow, shaved and washed and running around the dock in his pelt every morning. Will you look at him now, by Jesus! Thanks be to God, he's as filthy and as dirty as the filthiest and dirtiest of our own . . . and some of them not a million miles from us either! Wouldn't he soften the heart of a Jewman, the filthy poor fucker!'

Nature felt that it was up to him to take offence at this but someone shouted that the parade was coming and they all strained their ears to catch the strange music that gained strength and faded away again according as the procession negotiated the maze of twisting streets. Such a mixture of music was never before heard in Ballycastle. In a fit of anger and spite the Dockers Band refused to play anything but *Roll out the Barrel* which they kept belting out defiantly. Councillor Macken finally succeeded in getting the St Francis Xavier Brass Band to strike up the theme music from *Message of Fatima* but their nerve was almost gone and for love, money or the new Republic they couldn't turn into either of the other two tunes they knew. When the crowd in the Square saw and heard what was happening they squirmed with delight. They hadn't come in vain!

A small group of churchmen and other dignitaries sat on the platform to receive the parade; people whose dignity would not allow them to march with the Dockers Band. The Professor of Irish was there to read the Proclamation of 1916, his mortal enemy the Professor of Archaeology, who was already under the weather, Monsignor Blake who wanted to play football with the little boys and was being restrained by the Bishop's secretary. The Reverent Maxwell sat some distance away from this group looking lost and uncomfortable. Someone noticed his flies were open and this, and Monsignor Blake's struggle to escape from the Bishop's secretary, drew further comment.

'Well isn't he the terrible old ram!' said Michael Thornton. 'And at this hour of his life too! Ready to slap it into any class of old hairpin that would have him and no delay!'

'Here you!' said the Tailor to Nature. 'It's not here you should be standing scratching your balls, a man who fought a hundred battles, but up there on the platform with those heroes who died for Ireland. Up with you! Slap on your medals and decorations and take a place of honour. Maybe Councillor Macken will get you a military pension!'

'Look out for yourself, you that was got through a blanket or I'll shove your crutches up your. . . .'

'Language, boys! Blood an' ounce but remember the day that's in it,' shouted the Sergeant.

'Did you ever hear tell of the Black and Tan who fell into a ditch up there above on his way back to the barracks?' asked the Cook. 'Well, he fell on his hand-gun and shot himself in the stomach. When he was found in the morning there wasn't a thimble-full of blood left in him. As dry as a bloody cork he was. But I tell you that six men in this town are drawing IRA pensions for having shot him. They all swore they ambushed him and Old Macken gave them letters to prove it.'

The crowd roared laughing but the laughter was interrupted by a loud roar. It was the Pooka in one of his political frenzies.

'Will you look at him,' he shouted. 'Old Macken's son! Old Macken that was put on a shovel outside the door for three nights as a child because they thought he was a changeling! Old Macken that would lick salt off a corpse!'

'Oh, for the love of Jesus, lads,' said the Sergeant, 'have some frigging respect for the proclamation if you don't have it for anything else. They're going to unveil the Memorial.'

Councillor Macken pulled a tape and shouted into the microphone, 'I declare this Memorial open! Long live the Republic!' The Memorial was a rectangle of marble with an inscription in gold. The crowd around the platform clapped in such a half-hearted way that it annoyed the Councillor even more. Everything seemed to be going against him all day and he told the Professor of Irish abruptly to read the Proclamation. He was a small tubby man bursting with pomposity and self-importance. He faced the microphone and words began to spout out of him like porter out

133

of a barrel that had its tap removed suddenly. Anyone who wasn't very familiar with the Proclamation would be doing well to catch a word in ten. But as he neared the half-way mark another diversion occurred. From the moment the Memorial was unveiled the Professor of Archaeology had been kneeling in front of it examining every word of the inscription which he knew was composed by his enemy. Then right in the middle of the Proclamation he let out a triumphant whoop. 'A mistake! A mistake! Upon my solemn oath there's a mistake!'

The Professor of Irish stopped his mad sprint through the Proclamation as if he had been pole-axed, his mouth stayed open and he began to stare at the Memorial. The crowd rushed in from the sides of the Square and a great commotion began. Councillor Macken looked as if he might actually burst with rage.

'Show it to me!' screamed the Professor of Irish. 'Show it to me!' He was so stunned that he forgot he hadn't spoken to the other man for fifteen years. The Professor of Archaeology knew he owned the centre of the stage. He rose with some difficulty to his feet, walked to the Memorial and placed an unsteady finger on the last line of the inscription. *They fanned the flame of freedom alive.* He looked smugly at his enemy and shouted: 'To life! To life! To life!'

The Professor of Irish turned grey with sudden relief and renewed rage. He banged his copy of the Proclamation on the platform and began to screech and stamp his feet.

'Alive! Alive! Alive! You illiterate drunk! You broken-down mole! You. . . . Ah! Ah! Ah!'

'Arrah, hit him a belt, sir!' shouted the Pooka. 'Give him the hobnails! Out on fair-play with the two of you!'

Now the platform party got involved in the argument as some of them shouted 'Alive!' and others 'To life'. When Councillor Macken succeeded in calming the professors, Monsignor Blake surprised everybody by catching the microphone and quavering in the most comic way:

134

'Alive, Alive, O! Alive, Alive O!
Crying cockles and mussels, Alive, Alive O!'

and laughing and clapping himself loudly. When the Minister saw the Monsignor laughing he thought it safe to laugh himself although he hadn't the slightest idea what this new row was about. He neighed suddenly and unexpectedly, just as order was being restored, like a lost foal summoning his mother. Councillor Macken rounded on him, 'Shut your face you black Protestant lunatic!' Then he roared at the Dockers Band, 'Play the National Anthem, for the love and honour of God!' But their leader looked at him maliciously in the eye and said, 'Hadn't you better have a word with your beauties from the Third Order! We're dying of the drought!' He gave a signal to the band and they marched off silently to the Lobster Pot.

'Sing it yourself,' roared the crowd. 'Rise it like a good man! Think of our patriot dead!'

The St Francis Xavier Brass Band stood looking at one another sheepishly when the Bishop's secretary took charge of the situation and shouted to the young man in the broadcasting van to get a record immediately. The young man was enjoying the total confusion so much that he had to be twice nudged into action. He jumped into the back of the van and began to root among the records.

'Silence, you bloody jackasses!' shouted Councillor Macken. 'Silence for our National Anthem!'

This had an immediate effect and for the first time that day the Councillor was in complete control of a situation. But it was certainly not his day! In his blind rush the young man slapped the wrong record on the turntable and the now silent crowd heard the opening bars of the Ballycastle Céilí Band playing a lively jig. He whipped it off again but the damage was done. After that there was no possible recovery. The crowd cheered and began to dance, singly and in groups. The Pooka caught the Cook, swung him around and shouted, 'Another couple here for the Walls of Limerick! Around the house and mind the dresser!'

The crowd dispersed reluctantly but in high good humour. It had been a great occasion and would be discussed for many a day in the pubs of Ballycastle. Already Michael Thornton was conducting a discussion in the Corner Bar which he had hurriedly opened. But Sergeant Lynch stayed exactly where he was, his cheek turned to the sky examining the Memorial with one eye closed. Then he said to himself, 'It's all very peculiar. I can't make head or tale out of it.' He put his two feet on the pedals and cycled slowly home to his dinner.

4

Martin spent the evening scouring the town for news of Billy but to no avail. He called into Maggie's bar where he found Councillor Macken and the Fine Gael contingent downing rapid whiskeys and condemning the behaviour of the two professors, Monsignor Blake, the Reverend Maxwell, the Dockers Band and almost everyone else in the town who had contributed in any way to the débâcle at the Square. Martin tried to sneak a discreet word with Maggie but all she could tell him was that the baggage was still lying unclaimed and that nobody at all had called. But Councillor Macken caught sight of him and attacked.

'Be gone out of here, you dirty little Communist! You're not fit for decent company! You struck a priest and the striking hand will wither to the shoulder!'

Maggie asked him to be quiet but Martin told her not to mind him. The outburst had no effect at all on him other than that he found it rather amusing. He said goodbye to Maggie and resumed his search.

He then met a student from the town who told him he had seen Billy the previous night with a woman, walking towards Fiddler's Hill. This was where the guest house was where Billy had his Good Friday assignation. Martin didn't want to get too involved with any of Billy's women as they generally meant trouble of one kind or another. But he was anxious to see Billy as his mind was now firmly made up to go to England in the morning. And apart from friendship he was looking forward, in a peculiar way, to enjoying Billy's certain envy as well as his genuine sadness at the parting. But he resolved not to mention Stella Walsh at all.

He waited until darkness had fallen before he approached the Immaculate Guest House, a huge, rambling rookery where low-grade commercial travellers, lorry drivers and post office clerks took lodgings. Martin had never been inside the door but the owner, another MacDonough from Irishtown, had a wide reputation as a heavy drinker and pub brawler. When Martin came into the dimly lit hall he saw a small, dark-haired woman in her early thirties sitting in a little office reading a book with a lurid cover.

'I'm looking for a girl called Maisie? Would you be able to help me?'

But he was startled, and must have shown it clearly, when she said, in a most unfriendly manner, 'I'm Maisie! What do you want?'

'It's Billy, Billy O'Grady, do you know? I only want to find him!'

'Billy O'Grady? What Billy.? I don't know any O'Grady. . . .'

Martin knew he was trapped and did his best to escape but she came at him suddenly and caught him by the lapels. When she came near him he found it hard to believe that even Billy, with a bottle of whiskey on board, would go to bed with her. She was older than he had first thought and was plastered with cheap make-up. God knows, he thought, it was true what that man in the Lobster Pot said about the cracked plate!

'I have him now!' she said, tugging at him. 'Willie Hyde my arse! Now, if you meet him before I do will you tell him this much.' She was pressing against him angrily and he found her tobacco-laden breath stifling. He was saved by a cry from the staircase where the owner appeared in singlet and trousers, much the worse for drink.

'So you're getting up on the customers in the fucking hall now are you? The Lord save us and guard us but you're getting a right hammering these days. We'll have to get your arse riveted, God bless the mark! What class of a fish have you hooked this time?'

Martin broke her grip and ran out the door laughing loudly. He didn't stop running until he reached the Memorial on the Square where he found Sergeant Lynch sitting on his bicycle studying the inscription.

'Do you know, I'm inclined to think myself that it should be "to life" after all,' he said to Martin. 'I'm not able to make any sense out of it as it is. Ha?'

Martin asked him if he had seen Billy O'Grady during the past few days. He thought for a moment and said he hadn't seen him for over twenty-four hours but that he knew who could give him definite information and to come with him. They both walked towards a dance-hall on a far corner of the Square where a Monster Freedom Céilí and Old-time Waltzing was being held. It was a very rough dance-hall frequented mainly by soldiers, country people and servant girls in the town, most of whom came from the country. The Sergeant told him he had seen Billy two nights previously with a wardsmaid from the hospital, known locally as Red Cross Crabs, and that she was at the Monster Freedom Céilí. Having given him this piece of information the Sergeant began to sound him out about the fight with his brother and with Mrs Anderson but before he could make any headway a young policeman came sprinting towards them.

'Hurry! Hurry, Sergeant! They're at it in the dance-hall. Four soldiers are kicking the bejasus out of a crowd of country fellows. I don't know if it's about hurling or politics or women!'

The Sergeant took the news calmly, still pushing the bicycle forward by pressing his right foot against the ground.

'Ha? And what class of shoes were those soldiers wearing when they went in, did you notice?'

138

'Shoes?' said the young policeman. 'Shoes? They were wearing Army boots, of course!'

'Of course!' said the Sergeant sarcastically. 'Why wouldn't they! Isn't it well known that they are the very best kind of dancing-pump. This is the class of bright boys they're sending me out of the Depot these days. Did you ever see people dancing in hobnailed boots? Sure, Mother of divine Jesus wouldn't a child of six know that they were going in there to start a kicking-match.'

'Will we have to use our batons, Sergeant?' asked the young policeman nervously.

'No! No! We keep them for pleasuring the ladies but I'll tell you what you will do. Run down there and tell the band to keep playing a waltz or a reel-set or anything at all and then come out and tell me how the fight is going.'

As the young man ran back to the dance-hall two bottles came crashing through a window. The hall was situated over a garage and the only entrance was up a steep flight of stairs which led from the street door to the dance-hall door. Two men now stood at the top of the stairs kicking people, who tried to crash the dance while the fight was going on, down again to the front door. They were also casting down people who had been ejected from the hall by the force of the swirling mob. Three people lay groaning and bleeding on the footpath outside the door. The Sergeant ignored all this and gave Martin some advice.

'It's two bob to get in but you'll be able to buy a "pass-out" for a shilling . . . or even less after this racket. Good! The band is playing again. Now maybe!'

He placed his bicycle against the wall and walked carefully to the door, moving aside the groaning, bleeding bodies with his big boots. The young policeman came tearing down the stairs for further instructions. But before he could report on the progress of the fight, a group of men came charging around the corner led by the Kipeen Burke. The Sergeant stood in the entrance to the stairs, blocking it completely with his huge frame. The Kipeen stood in front of him.

'Stand aside now, Sergeant! There are Free State soldiers up there kicking lads from our village. Let us up the stairs!'

The Sergeant raised his hand and addressed the Kipeen and his followers officially. 'Nobody is going up that stairs until the fight is over. That's the length and breadth of it now in any bloody language you like. There's only one way in or out and anybody who went up that stairs must come down again at some time. That's simple and natural!'

The Kipeen took off his cap and dashed it to the ground, he did the same with his jacket and his jersey. Then he leaped in the air and let out a roar that could be heard over all the din in the dance-hall.

'If you were four times as big and four times as bulky you wouldn't keep me from my kinsmen. We have respect for you, more than we have for anyone else in the force, but if you don't stand aside the boots will be put into you and we'll trample all over you and get in despite you. Now, for the last time, stand aside! Get out of that door!'

The young policeman had turned ashen and was about to draw his baton when an explosion shook the town. Windows in the dance-hall were blown out and slates rained down off the roofs of houses all round the Square. Shanahan had blown up the Memorial.

The Sergeant grabbed his bicycle and shouted to the young policeman to follow him. He cursed under his breath for having left the Memorial to go to the dance-hall. A crowd followed him and another came screaming down the stairs from the dance-hall. People could be heard running towards the Square from all sides but the upper half of the Square, where the Memorial had stood, was in complete darkness. All the street lights were shattered and nothing at all was left of the Memorial save a hole in the ground where it had stood. Nothing much of Shanahan was left either. He caught the full force of the blast and only his head, which was found on the far side of the Square wasn't completely fragmented. The Sergeant ordered the crowd to stand back, which they readily did when they saw the young policeman getting violently ill. There was a

140

terrible silence over the whole town and the people on the Square didn't dare speak above a whisper.

'Poor old bastard!' said the Sergeant. 'His guts and his flesh will have to be scraped off the street with spoons. Why the hell didn't he take a twelve-pound sledgehammer to it?'

Martin felt sickened and disturbed and was glad he had already made his mind up to go. He turned away in disgust from the curious, prying crowd and walked rapidly towards the Four Masters Hotel. The bar was packed with people shouting for large whiskies and giving garbled and inaccurate accounts of what had happened. One man kept on announcing loudly that it was the Kipeen Burke who had set off the bomb. Another time Martin would have been in the thick of it with his own story, but now he felt no urge to deny even the wildest rumour. He saw Larry in a corner of the lounge but he didn't recognise the girl who was serving in the bar and there was no sign of Stella. He greeted Larry.

'Well, it's all settled at last. I'm going over to see Mary and I'll see what will happen after that. I had a terrible fight with my brother but now I'm just as pleased it happened.'

Larry clapped him on the shoulder. 'We'll have a drink on that and then we'll hit the road. I'm driving to Dublin tonight. As soon as my pilot heard about the poor devil on the Square he began to talk about firing parties and guards of honour so I let him go. It's a bad business. I knew by his eyes that night that he had something desperate in mind. May the Lord have mercy on him!' Larry raised his glass and drank.

'He'd have done as much damage to it with a twelve-pound sledge,' said Martin and no sooner had he said it than he felt ashamed; neither the words nor the sentiments were his own. Larry shrugged his shoulders impatiently.

'That kind of talk is a bit too easy. The trouble with this country is that we always seem to be about a hundred years behind ourselves, not to mention others. I sometimes think we lost too much and that we'll never never make up for it.'

He was silent for a while as he stared into his glass. Then he drained it and started his sudden crab-like walk to the door, speaking over his shoulder to Martin.

'The bill's paid and the bags are in the car. I met your little girl on my way in and she gave me a hint about your plans. She also gave me this.'

He handed Martin a little box and in a half-joking, half-serious way asked, 'Was she good to you, Martin?' Martin got confused and blushed and then got angry at the bluntness of the question. But it only lasted an instant and he said, 'Yes, Larry, she was indeed!'

Larry placed his hands firmly on Martin's shoulders and, looking directly into his eyes, said, 'I'm sorry if I offended you! I wasn't just being curious but I am a cussed fellow in many ways. But I want to tell you I think you're on the right road, if you protect yourself against the world and learn to think for yourself. Don't ever let anyone spancel you against your will and don't let this bitch of a country spancel you either.'

He turned away to open the door of the car, but Martin thought he noticed a moistness in the eyes for the first time since he met him. He opened the little box and found a tiny model car with a note wrapped around it.

'Just to remind you of the "powerful engine". Write if you have time and we might meet again some time. Mind yourself. I'm very fond of you.'

He laughed to himself and thought what a pity it was they hadn't met sooner. But later as he sat silently beside Larry, thinking of the future, Ballycastle receded farther and farther into the past.